NO SHRINKING VIOLET

THE LILLYMOUTH MYSTERIES

BOOK TWO

R. A. Hutchins

Cover Design by Thia Whitten at PixelSquirrel

ISBN: 9798397357876

For Andrew, who is about to go out into the world, I couldn't be more proud xx

Other Murder Mystery Titles by this Author:

Baker's Rise Mysteries -
Here Today, Scone Tomorrow
Pie Comes Before A Fall
Absence Makes the Heart Grow Fondant
Muffin Ventured, Muffin Gained
Out with the Old, In with the Choux
All's Fair in Loaf and War
A Walk In the Parkin
The Jam Before the Storm
Things Cannoli Get Better
A Stitch In Key Lime (November 2023)

CAST OF CHARACTERS

ARCHIE – Mynah bird

CATHY BARNES – Local baker

STAN BARNES – Local baker

DAISY BLOOM – New parish vicar

WENDY BLOOM (DECEASED) – Daisy's grandmother

COUNCILLOR BARRY BRIDGES – Local councillor

MARTHA BRIDGES – Wife of local councillor, on parish council

ROBERT BRIGGS SENIOR – Local landowner of Briggs' Farm

MAGGIE BUCKLEY – Sylvia's friend, works at Tourist Information office.

GERALD BUNCH – Local florist

RON CARMICHAEL (DECEASED) – Sylvia's husband

SYLVIA CARMICHAEL – Wendy Bloom's best friend, Vicarage Housekeeper

DETECTIVE INSPECTOR RHYS CLUERO – Local detective

GEMMA DALTON (NEE SANDERSON) – Co-owner of local pub, the Crow's Nest Inn

PAUL DALTON – Gemma's husband, works at Briggs' Farm

ENVIRONMENTAL ACTIVISTS – Jugger, Badger, Tallie, and Aislin

ANDREW FREEMAN – Bea's husband, joiner

BEA (ABIGAIL) FREEMAN – Owner of Bea's Book Nook and Daisy's best friend

DAISY MAE FREEMAN – Daughter of Bea and Andrew

ANTHONY GLENDINNING – Son of Violet and Percy

PERCY GLENDINNING – Local bank manager

VIOLET GLENDINNING – Wife of Percy, head of parish council

DANIEL HARPER – Bea's dad

MORAG HARPER – Bea's mum

JACOB – Vicarage cat

BUGSY MALONE – Sylvia's house rabbit

REVEREND MARTIN – Daisy's predecessor

DETECTIVE INSPECTOR MICHELLE MATLOCK – Local detective

JOE (JOSEPH) PIERCE – Café owner at 'The Boatyard'

BILLY SANDERSON – Co-owns the Crow's Nest Inn with his daughter Gemma.

MILDRED SPRATT – Church organist

LYDIA STANLEY – Works in planning department at local council offices

TERRY STEWART – Local Policeman

ROSEMARY WESSEX – Local librarian

CONTENTS

1. A VICAR ON THE BRINK OF BREAKDOWN

Reverend Daisy woke up with a start, her hair plastered to her forehead and her pyjamas clinging to her body which was drenched in sweat from the nightmare. An all-too regular occurrence now, Daisy had tried everything to have a more peaceful night's sleep – from lavender pillow spray to herb-infused cocoa before bed – yet so far nothing had worked. Her mind was determined to relive the final twenty-four hours of her grandmother's life from their final argument to Daisy's discovery of the broken body in the florist shop, the vase used in the attack lying blood-splattered and cracked by her grandmother's legs. And the whole thing so real, the feelings evoked so terrifying even in her dream state that Daisy's body was now on the verge of yet another panic attack. Daisy gulped down water from the glass on her bedside table and checked her phone for the time. Half past three. It was like clockwork.

The vicar's turbulent nocturnal patterns were, however, not enough to dissuade – or even awaken – the large, solid lump of ginger fur who snored now at the foot of the bed. Until she had sat up quickly, Jacob must've been resting on Daisy's feet, as she could feel the tingle as the blood rushed back into her toes. She turned on her lamp and took in the now familiar surroundings of her room in the small vicarage. All remnants of Daisy's predecessor's penchant for exercise had long since been removed, and in their place stood a modern bookshelf and a comfortable reading chair covered in cushions and blankets. Daisy valued this calm and quiet retreat more than she let on to Sylvia, her housekeeper, who preferred a constant background noise of cop shows and chatter.

As she did every night at this time, Daisy took out the pretty cloth-covered journal which had been a Christmas present from her best friend Bea last month. She pulled up her duvet as far as the heavy weight of the cat at the bottom of the bed would allow, once again silently cursing the diocese which was taking so long to have central heating installed in the old place.

A large cooking range in the kitchen and an open fire in the sitting room were great for warming those rooms in the daytime, but it had so far been a long, cold winter otherwise. *And not just because of the temperatures,* Daisy thought sadly, reading for the umpteenth time the stilted, formal note in the front of the book, so unlike the Bea she used to know.

Whilst their friendship had thawed slightly since Daisy outed Robert Briggs Senior and his underhand methods regarding building a new resort at his farm, thus indirectly causing Bea's husband to lose the lucrative joinery contract they had been banking on, things were still frosty between the two women. The sadness resulting from their estrangement was like a ball of ice in Daisy's chest, and she had shed more than a few tears on the subject. Bea had been civil, of course, and had served Daisy in the tearoom at the back of her bookshop with the same pleasantness as any other customer, accepting the presents for her daughter, little Daisy Mae politely – but seemingly not seeing them as the peace offerings which Daisy intended them to be. The vicar knew she would need to have a more direct conversation if their friendship were to be saved, but she had yet to build up the courage. Instead, she wrote everything she wished to share with Bea in the journal, her writing decorated by splodges of tears in the dark of the night.

Not for the first time, Daisy thought about starting a
'journalling for wellness' group in the church hall, and
made a mental note to actually do something about it
this coming week. Right now, though, she really
needed some more sleep, especially as tomorrow
(*today?*) was Sunday and not only was Daisy preaching
at the morning service, but she would also require all
of her acting skills. Today was the last Sunday in the
month and therefore the morning on which Gerald
Bunch would publicly profess his undying love for the
parish incumbent, ending with a seemingly heartfelt
offer of marriage. Of course, between the two of them,
they both knew the whole thing was a charade, but the
man had saved Daisy's life when she had first returned
to Lillymouth, and in return she was bound to
perpetuate the image of him as a lecherous buffoon. In
reality, in the few private conversations they had since
shared, Bunch had proven himself to be a highly
intelligent and sensitive man, who Daisy felt she could
call on if she needed sensible advice. As to what his
real purpose in the town was – or his real name for that
matter – Daisy was, however, still firmly in the dark.

This was not the only area in which the truth eluded
Daisy. In the six months since she had been back in
Lillymouth, the vicar had failed to find any tangible

clue that would lead to her uncovering her grandmother's murderer, the criminal having gone undetected for over fifteen years now. A fact which vexed her greatly. No, Daisy's time was instead taken up with refereeing parish council meetings, with avoiding the still furious Robert Briggs who had thankfully been asked to step down from his own role on that council and with thwarting the man's attempts to oust her from the parish. All of that along with the usual church services, funerals, weddings and blessings that her vocation required, meant that Daisy was very busy indeed.

Other than a very sad series of events up at the Bayview Hotel in the autumn time, however, the town had settled down to its winter slumber with little more of note to mention. Christmas had come and gone in an exhausting flurry of church services and visits which had further contributed to Daisy's exhaustion, meaning that now she was very much a vicar on the brink of breakdown.

Something had to give, but what?

2. YOU'LL NEED A PEG FOR YOUR NOSE

"I'm telling you, Vicar, they have to go!" Violet Glendinning's petulant and shrieky tone grated on Daisy's last nerve and, not for the first time that evening, she made an obvious point of checking her watch and yawning out loud.

"I agree." Billy Sanderson, co-owner of the Crow's Nest Inn with his daughter Gemma, sat with his arms folded across his large beer belly, leaning back on the small wooden chair to the point that Daisy wondered whether the back or legs of the ancient seat would give out first.

With a sigh, Daisy prepared herself to reiterate the point she had already made three times in this parish council meeting alone, "They are doing no harm. They simply want to protest the fossil fuels used in the steam train and the air pollution caused by using such locomotives. They see it as a step backwards." In truth, Daisy had no idea why a group of high profile environmental activists would want to pitch up in their little town, protesting against a small engine which would only pull one carriage of sightseers a mile along the coastal track and back a few times a day in the summer months. *Surely there must be more pressing causes?*

"When in reality it's a step in the right direction, back to the traditional ways of the town, which should be our main selling point with tourists anyway – come and enjoy a slice of the old-fashioned way of life," Violet nodded her head vigorously to agree with her own point and removed an invisible piece of fluff from her cardigan.

The vicar refrained from voicing her personal thoughts on the matter, but did make the final point which she knew would silence the very vocal Mrs. Glendinning – for the moment at least, "Anyway, Violet, it was your Anthony who told the group about the town when he met them at that festival down south in September, wasn't it? So perhaps you need to be discussing it a bit closer to home and seeing if he can get them to move on."

The comment had the desired effect, and Violet clamped her mouth shut, her eyes firing invisible daggers at Daisy and her thin lips pursed so tightly as to have almost disappeared.

"That little train will bring my pub a lot of extra business, the station being just up the lane from us," Billy insisted on having the last word, "as well as increasing revenue for a lot of the other businesses in this town. The Lottery grant funding is there, we've sourced an engine and carriage from the locomotive museum in Durham, we need to move on with the project without these hippies holding it up any longer."

Daisy wasn't sure what to address first – the prejudice inherent in the man's remark or the fact that 'moving on' with the project was obviously never going to be simple, very few things in this town were, she was finding – instead she tut tutted loudly at his use of terminology for the activists and began gathering up her things. Her head was pounding along with her leg and hip and Daisy wanted nothing more than a long, hot soak in the bath with her latest choice of historical fiction.

"I'll speak to my Barry and find out what stage the

town council are at with the whole thing," Martha Bridges, wife of the local town councillor and always the one to pour oil on troubled waters, rounded off the conversation, earning her a grateful smile from Daisy.

"Thank you, Martha, and I'll go up to the old station and speak to them," Daisy offered, though in reality she'd rather do anything but.

"You'll need a peg for your nose," Violet said harshly, "since they moved into the original waiting room it smells like a pigsty."

"Joyful," Daisy muttered under her breath as she limped out, her cane tapping angrily on the parquet floor.

"There's a brew in the pot," Sylvia called over the jarring sounds of a police chase on the television in the sitting room as Daisy entered the vicarage.

Oh for an evening without the background noise of international crime, Daisy thought to herself, choosing the opposite direction to the kitchen and hobbling along to her bedroom. Without comment, she bent down and picked up her books and papers from the floor beside her bed and replaced them on the night stand. Jacob looked at her from the corner of his eye, no doubt hoping for some sort of reaction, but Daisy refused to give the silly animal any satisfaction. This game of swiping her things onto the floor whilst the vicar was out was wearing very thin, and certainly tonight was not the time to engage in their usual 'discussion' on the matter.

Huffing at the lack of response, the cat stood slowly from his spot on Daisy's pillow – the large indent of his body having almost flattened that cushion completely – stretched, yawned and then swiped at Daisy's backpack with a fat paw for good measure.

"Hey, I just put that down," Daisy couldn't catch the words before they were out, and was annoyed to see the smug smile of satisfaction that graced the creature's lips at her reaction.

"Finally! Knew I'd get you in the end!" Daisy could imagine the cat saying, further fuelling her irritation. In a move which she was certain her back and hip would make her pay for in the morning, Daisy scooped the hefty feline into her arms. Caught unawares, Jacob let out a yowl of protest, but it was too late, Daisy was already limping back towards the kitchen, steadfastly refusing to release the hissing, squirming orange bundle. Breathing heavily and no longer steady on her

feet, the vicar deposited the animal unceremoniously in his cat bed in the boot room – much to the amusement of Archie the mynah bird, who made the sound of a cell door shutting to further add insult to injury. His repertoire had expanded threefold in the time since Sylvia had moved in, mostly sounds and phrases picked up from the housekeeper's viewing habits, and Daisy couldn't honestly say that she approved. Quite the opposite in fact, and so the vicar had been trying to teach the bird some Bible phrases whenever she had a moment. The resulting amalgamation of the two input streams, she had to admit, had been somewhat shocking.

Closing the door firmly on the pair, hoping she wouldn't have to drink her tea to the sounds of fur and feathers flying, Daisy sank down onto a chair at the farmhouse style kitchen table. Caught up in her thoughts, she lifted the unnecessarily heavy, utilitarian teapot and poured herself a drink into the mug which Sylvia had left out for her, all the while trying to tune out the sounds of her housemates. What with the lack of sleep, Briggs' vendetta against her, the demands of the parish, and the poor state of her relationship with Bea, Daisy felt the weight of the world on her shoulders. Worse still, her brain often felt so foggy it was hard to think the issues through logically, let alone decide how to act upon them.

Too tired to cry, Daisy simply prayed for guidance, for some sort of breakthrough and for the knowledge to know what to do when it came. In the meantime, she knew, she'd have to keep trying, no matter the personal cost.

3. FRIAR TUCK

The cold, Northern air seemed to settle in Daisy's
bones at this time of year, making her aches all the
more intolerable, and the next day was particularly
cold. A brisk, icy wind from the East came across the
Bay and was no doubt the reason why the vicar saw
barely a soul on her journey to the old train station
after breakfast. Situated on the other side of the
Lillywater river, the two platforms had once been on
the now defunct coastal line from Whitby, which had
travelled through Staithes and eventually ended in
Redcar. The track had been decommissioned in the '70s
though, and the once bustling buildings had fallen into
a state of disrepair.

Raised voices greeted Daisy's arrival at what was once

a cosy waiting room and the vicar hovered outside on the platform, not wanting to interrupt. Of course, she couldn't help but eavesdrop a little, given the volume of the decidedly heated conversation.

"You're a chauvinistic pig! And one who won't man up to his responsibilities at that!" A woman's voice penetrated the thin antique glass of the three windows which formed the side of the building.

"And you wouldn't know what was best for you if it slapped you in the face! Which is what I've got a good mind to do..." An angry male voice retorted, just as the old wooden door slammed open, causing Daisy to jump and sending a smattering of dry paint flakes and splinters of wood flying into the air. A small, red-headed young woman emerged, sparing barely a glance at the vicar before she stomped off in the direction of the car park. She wore a fleece jacket which seemed to swamp her petite frame and had a knitted hat pulled low on her forehead so as to make her eyes barely visible.

"Tallie! Get back here! Right now, or there'll be trouble!" A large body filled the doorframe, making Daisy take an unconscious step back along the platform. Seeing the vicar, the man ran his fingers through his long, unwashed hair, scowling aggressively, "What do you want? I've had my fill of do-gooders and naysayers in this blasted town. And if it's Bible bashing you've come for, you can..."

"Actually, I just wanted a chat," Daisy forced herself to speak up, though her internal alarm bells were ringing. She had met many agitated, angry people in her former profession – both men and women – and Daisy had learned the hard way to tread very carefully. Very carefully indeed.

"A chat?" He asked, an incredulous sneer overtaking his otherwise unremarkable features, "I'm not in the business of holding mothers' meetings over tea and cake, Vicar." The man nodded at Daisy's dog collar, and the vicar felt the blush rise from under the apparently offensive article and straight up her cheeks.

"To discuss your plans," Daisy continued, more shakily still, "since this is town property and you are trespassing." She regretted the last words as soon as she'd spoken them, as the man seemed to rear up to his full height, gripping the feeble doorframe with a white-knuckled grasp.

"Bog off and go tend to your flock or something," the man said, advancing on Daisy, "we've got squatters' rights and legitimate concerns regarding environmental protection."

Unbeknownst to him, Daisy had quite a wide knowledge on his alleged rights and stood her ground, though her heart was beating almost out of her chest and her breathing had the shallow beginnings of a panic attack, "Hmm, I'll have the local constable pay a visit then. Perhaps you'd rather chat with him."

"Is he a cripple too?" He jeered, "Do what you like, you women are all the same, whining and complaining."

"Well, aren't you a delight," Daisy forced a clearly fake smile, pressing on, "Daisy Bloom, parish vicar." It was a bit late for pleasantries, but she was keen to know the man's name so that she could speak to Anthony Glendinning and hopefully find out his story. Or, even better, have a police background check run on him.

"Friar Tuck," he replied, clearly pleased with himself and displaying a set of yellowing, chipped teeth.

Daisy couldn't tell if the bloke was actually in his forties or if he just had a prematurely aged appearance, either way she was about to turn and leave when another man appeared in the doorway.

"Oy Jugger, got any scran?" This man was significantly thinner and, Daisy thought, could do with a hearty meal.

"Perhaps our good vicar here would like to invite us to the vicarage for tea and scones?" The burly man nicknamed Jugger cast a final look of scorn in Daisy's direction before pushing past his companion to return inside.

"Do you?" this new man asked, eying Daisy with displeasure, his gaze travelling the length of her in slow perusal.

"Do I what?" Daisy asked, trying to keep the wobble from her voice.

"Give out free scran at that vicarage of yours."

"Oh! Well, ah, if someone in real need turned up, then yes, ah, I suppose..."

The man twisted his thin face as he processed this information, never once taking his eyes off her.

"Get back in here and leave the poor woman alone, Badger," a female voice came from behind him then, and Daisy had to admit to being thankful for the arrival of another woman.

The man named Badger gave the vicar a thoughtful nod as he turned on his heel and disappeared. A cheerful looking woman took his place, older than the men it seemed, her greying hair scraped up into a brightly coloured headscarf and her round cheeks ruddy with the cold, "Aislin, nice to meet you love," she held out a hand covered in a knitted fingerless glove that had seen better days, and Daisy moved forward to shake it.

"Daisy Bloom, local vicar, I was just wanting to see how you're all doing. You must be freezing."

"Aye well, the lads have got a fire going in the old grate and we've a camping stove to boil water on for drinks. We're used to it."

"Do you do a lot of activism in small towns, I mean, over seemingly small issues like this? Are you part of a bigger organisation?" Daisy asked, hoping to get the name of a larger group she could search up on the internet so as to get a better insight into their intentions and the likely duration of their protest.

A shadow passed over the woman's face. Daisy had come across all types of folks in all types of situations in her years as a victim liaison officer, and she was sure she wasn't mistaken – that was guilt she saw in Aislin's expression before it was swiftly hidden back behind her cheery façade.

"We go where we need to," was the cryptic response, and it was clear she was shutting down further conversation. The woman crossed her arms over her bosom and was about to turn away before she paused and quietly added, "You seem like a nice lady. If I were you, vicar, I wouldn't get involved. Don't ask questions, don't come looking again, for your own sake."

Was that a threat?

As Aislin disappeared inside, Daisy took her first full breath of the past few minutes, focusing on regulating her breathing and calming the dizziness that threatened to overtake her.

Well that was anything but productive, she thought to herself, *I've likely made things worse by getting their backs up and rousing suspicion.*

Daisy made her way back to her car as quickly as her body could manage, dodging the decades-old potholes and surprised to see the young woman from earlier still in the car park. Sitting on a half-collapsed bench at the side of the space, she was being comforted by another man who looked suspiciously like Anthony Glendinning. The vicar dared give them nothing but a swift glance, keen to avoid another confrontation, so simply stored the interesting crumb of information away for later as she searched for her car keys in her pocket and beat a hasty retreat.

Desperate for some caffeine and painkillers, Daisy deliberated for a moment before turning right on Front Street and parking outside Bea's Book Nook at the bottom of Cobble Wynd. Under no illusions that her friend would be happy to see her, Daisy was determined to persevere with saving their relationship. The winter months had done little to help Bea's already declining business, and Daisy was shocked to find the place freezing cold when she entered. Half of the lights along the dark, Victorian bookshelves were off, plunging the place into even more gloom than the single front window might suggest. What was worse, the large open fire in the tea nook at the back was unlit – something unheard of in this season in all the years Daisy had known the place.

"Bea?" Daisy shuffled through the dim shop, the whole atmosphere of the space making her feel even more unwelcome, "Bea are you here?" Worried that something might have happened, for surely only an emergency would cause her friend to leave the book shop door unlocked and the till unmanned for anyone to get their hand in, Daisy hurried the last few steps, stopping short when she saw someone hunched down on the closest leather armchair. "Bea, is that you?" Daisy asked again, anxiously waiting the few foreboding seconds before a small voice said, "Yes, of course it's me, what do you want, Daisy?"

The vicar let out a sigh of relief and rushed around to the other side, wanting to be able to see her friend's face, "Bea, what has happened? Where's Daisy Mae? Is she okay?"

"Of course she is, Andrew has taken her to the park. He's nothing better to do, after all," the clipped, bitter tone was not lost on Daisy, yet she sat down heavily on the nearest sofa and put down her cane and bag silently.

"Good, good, it's a bit chilly out there... and in here. Would you like me to light the fire?"

"No."

"I'll get us some hot drinks then and we can have a chat," Daisy was nothing if not persistent and when no negative response came she took that as her cue to go ahead.

The frosty silence persisted even after the vicar had placed both drinks on the table in front of them, however, so she decided to bite the bullet this time and stop tiptoeing around the elephant in the room as she had been doing for the past few months.

"So, business obviously isn't good," Daisy began, "and

Andrew is still looking for new joinery contracts. I'm guessing people don't tend to renovate over the winter. I'm sorry Bea. I'm so sorry that Andrew's business was affected when I outed Briggs and his underhand ways. It was never my intention, but you must understand I thought he was a murderer when I made all that information public. Perhaps the proposed development will still go ahead once he's had the bat survey? Maybe they won't find any evidence of roosting?"

"No, Daisy, no, the whole thing is off the table now, as Violet so delighted in telling me the other week. Why on earth that woman thinks it's her God-given right to stick her nose in everybody's business... and that husband of hers for telling her everything that goes on at the bank... anyway, apparently it's immaterial what the survey shows now, as Briggs' investors have pulled out because of all the bad publicity. I guess we just have to wait for the next big project to start right on our doorstep, because we both know how likely that is," Bea let out a bitter, sarcastic laugh that was so unlike the woman that Daisy used to know.

"Bea," Daisy whispered, shocked at the venom in the eyes that stared back at her, "Bea, can't we draw a line under it and go back to being friends?"

"I don't have time for drawing Daisy, I'm waiting for the estate agent to turn up to value this place so it can go on the market."

"No!" Daisy spoke loudly this time, knowing as she did that the book shop had been in Bea's family since Victorian times and was her friend's pride and joy, "There must be a way, Bea. I'll help you, I promise I will. Just let me think about it for a few days, see what I can come up with…"

"It's too late, vicar," Bea said, turning her back on Daisy and resuming the position in which she had been found, her coffee going cold on the table in front of them.

Wanting to reach out and hug her friend, but knowing the affection wouldn't be welcomed, Daisy tried to discreetly scrub at the tears which flowed down her cheeks as she put her winter coat back on and left the place… feeling as though she had left a part of her heart behind too.

4. A FAKE REACTION

Instead of returning to the vicarage, Daisy parked on
Church Street and let herself into the church by the
side entrance, hoping to have some moments for quiet
prayer and reflection. She had barely managed to
compose herself on the short drive up from the Book
Nook, and didn't want to encourage any of Sylvia's
gentle questioning as to why she was upset.

Surprised to find the lights on in the main chapel,
Daisy remembered too late that this was the day that
Gerald Bunch normally did the church flowers. Not
that she minded meeting him now – the opposite was
true, in fact, and she often found the man's insights
very useful – but Daisy had come here specifically to
avoid company.

"Vicar," Bunch spoke in the gentle tone that was reserved for her alone, Daisy being the only one who knew his secret – and yet didn't at the same time. Certainly, she knew he was not the man he purported to be publicly.

"Gerald," Daisy acknowledged him with a watery smile, hoping she could slip past where he worked at the main pulpit and disappear through the back to her small office where she had some chocolate stashed in the desk drawer.

"Daisy," he stepped slightly to the side to block her path, his expression worried.

"I'm okay, I'm okay," Daisy rushed out, feeling her eyes begin to leak again, "just a bad morning."

"Would you like to tell me about it?" His kindness was her undoing and Daisy found herself nodding her head whilst she walked into the man's open arms and the hug which he offered.

They stood there awkwardly for a few moments, Bunch leaning at a harsh angle to accommodate the vicar's much shorter stature, and she surprising herself by resting her head on the man's chest and allowing herself to switch off for a moment. This was the first time they had ever embraced – had so much as touched even – since the night he had carried her to the vicarage door last year. Daisy had to admit it wasn't unpleasant, being consoled like this for the first time in a very long time.

Finally, they pulled apart even more awkwardly, and without speaking moved to sit on the front pew.

Bunch sat sideways on the narrow bench, removed the silly spectacles from the end of his nose – which Daisy doubted he even really needed anyway – and gave the vicar his full attention, "A bad morning, you said?"

In words that at first came haltingly and then flowed faster as if a dam had burst, Daisy detailed her encounters at the train station and then with Bea. Not once did Bunch interrupt or question, he simply listened, nodded and took Daisy's hand in his when she broke down after describing her best friend's demeanour towards her.

"That sounds like a very bad morning," Bunch said gently, "and in my opinion you certainly don't deserve the way Bea has treated you these past months. It's a credit to your own lovely character that you've persevered. As for your encounter at the train station, perhaps it might be worth my while having a little wander up there this evening..."

"No, Gerald, don't put yourself in harm's way. If they can mock and threaten a disabled woman of the cloth, goodness knows what they'll do to you. I'm going to speak to the police. I just hoped gentle diplomacy might work in the first instance."

"Hmm," Bunch was noncommittal and changed the subject back to the book shop, "perhaps you can text Bea's mum and ask her to pop over. Whitby did you say her parents live?"

"Yes, her dad is the chief constable for North Yorkshire police force there."

"Well, maybe they're overdue a visit. You can't take it all on your shoulders, Daisy."

In the exact same moment they both realised their hands were still clasped together and both gave a small laugh to cover their embarrassment as they let go.

Daisy felt the loss of his warmth and judging by the look on Bunch's face, and the way he ran his thumb over the palm where the vicar's hand had been, he felt the same.

"Let me walk you back to Buttercup Cottage," Bunch always used the original name for the vicarage, having told Daisy previously that he had researched the history of the florist's shop and found that the florist in 1910 had married the vicar at the time and so had named the cottage after both her previous vocation and the small yellow flowers that were wont to spring up on the vicarage lawn. Daisy loved the story and the name, and intended to get a small name plaque for above the vicarage door in the springtime.

"No, no, Sylvia will be expecting me for lunch anyway, I just popped in here to collect myself a bit. She's lovely, but ah…" Daisy searched for a suitably diplomatic term.

"A bit suffocating? In your face?" Gerald laughed as Daisy nodded.

"Ah yes, perhaps best in small doses, not that I mean to be unkind, but she's definitely an extrovert whereas I'm…"

"An introvert," Bunch smiled down at her and Daisy allowed herself for a moment to bask in the feeling of being understood.

"Exactly," she let out a long breath and picked up her things, "anyway, see you later Gerald."

"See you later," he whispered as the vicar walked off, she herself wondering what exactly had just happened.

Daisy slumped down in the armchair in her bedroom some two hours later. She had returned to the vicarage to find Uncle Joe there, apparently having popped round to see her and then been invited to stay for lunch by Sylvia. He only opened his Boatyard coffee shop on Thursdays, Fridays and Saturdays in the winter months and so had more free time than usual. Now, Daisy didn't generally mind unexpected visitors – it was a vicarage after all – but she had known the exact reaction she was about to get when she told the pair she'd been to visit the group of environmental activists at the train station, and she hadn't been wrong.

So, here she sat, her stomach full of Sylvia's homemade leek and potato soup, and feeling duly chastised as if she was a child that had come home after curfew to face her parents. She had managed to sit through the lunch and then another pot of tea, said a grumpy goodbye to Joe and then had retreated to her room, only remembering at the last minute to thank her housekeeper for the food. Churlish indeed, though Daisy couldn't bring herself to regret her attitude – she was free to visit whomever she chose after all. Besides, she was the parish vicar, it was her job to intercede between clashing groups within the community.

Daisy stroked the fat cat on her lap who had launched

himself onto her laptop the moment she had sat down with it on her knees. Of course, Daisy knew she wasn't really going to get any work done right now anyway, not in her current mood – and if she was totally honest with herself, it wasn't all down to the conversation over lunch. Daisy felt conflicted and confused after her embrace with Bunch. She had, of course, told herself on repeat that he had simply caught her at a particularly emotional moment, that she was tired and running on empty. Probably her blood sugar was low. Deep down though, she knew she had felt something, some fluttering of butterflies in her stomach when the man held her that she'd had no business to be feeling, and Daisy was angry with herself because of that. She had sworn off men. Years ago. And had never once regretted that decision. Not that she regretted it now. *I mean,* she told herself sternly, *I likely don't even know the man's name. It was merely a fake reaction in a fake relationship.*

So why had it felt so real?

5. TUNA IS OFF THE TABLE

Daisy woke the next morning with a pulsing migraine over her left eye. The kind that makes moving your head, even a little, likely to cause vomiting. She huffed out a silent growl of exasperation and gritted her teeth, trying to roll onto her side so as to use her small stepladder to get down from the ridiculously high bed left from her predecessor. As if sensing her distress, Jacob appeared from the bottom of the bed, climbed onto Daisy's blanket-covered hip nonchalantly, despite the sharp intake of pain which she sucked through her teeth, and belly crawled up her body to rest splayed on his stomach across her chest. Once there, he paused, as if assessing the extent of Daisy's malaise and, having apparently decided the vicar needed some help waking herself for the day, the ginger tom cat then lifted one of his fat paws and promptly slapped her across the cheek with it.

Too stunned to move, in too much pain to shift the dead weight of the animal, especially in her prone position, Daisy opened one eye and whispered, "Tuna is… Off. The. Table… for the rest of this week." Despite her housekeeper's tutting, Daisy had taken to feeding the cat the odd treat of his favourite fishy delicacy. Well, more than the odd treat if she was honest. He had her wrapped around his oversized paw, that was for sure.

Well, no more, Daisy thought, as the assertive feline continued to stare at her languidly, before using the same paw to tap her chin three times in quick succession.

"Well!" Daisy exclaimed, having not been quick enough to jerk her head out of the way in time. Even that single word, uttered too loudly for her delicate state, rolled around like a marble in her head, "Get off! You, you…" Daisy was at a loss for a suitable insult, hoisting the top half of her body into an upright position. This had the desired result of effectively throwing the cat off to the side of her, but also the rather unfortunate side effect of causing the nausea to rise up her throat so fast that Daisy had to make an

inelegant dart for the small china sink against the far
wall. Of course, her hip and back protested this sudden
and injurious movement, adding to the vicar's extreme
discomfort as she began retching. The cat, who had
landed effortlessly on the blanket to the side of Daisy's
body when she sat up, seemed pleased with this
outcome, snuggling himself in a pretzel shape on the
vicar's still-warm pillow and closing his eyes in
contentment.

Spending the day in bed was simply not an option, so
Daisy washed down her prescription migraine and
pain medication with half a pot of Yorkshire tea, made
noncommittal grunts to Sylvia in response to her
questions about their evening meal, and dressed all in
black – an unusual occurrence for the woman who was
usually attracted to colour. At least, she normally tried
to give the impression of friendliness and
approachability to her parishioners, and bright fabrics
were one tactic which Daisy employed to aid her in
this effort. Not today though. No, today Daisy wanted
to simply fade into the background. To keep her
scheduled appointments with the minimum fuss or
attention. She had sent a text message to Bea's mum,
Morag, the night before, explaining that Bea seemed to
be in a bit of a bad way, and had agreed to meet the
woman this morning in the town park to have a walk

and a chat, maybe even to form a plan of action to help the family of three, before Morag visited Bea herself.

Daisy was looking forward to the fresh sea air and had always liked the small, green area which was bordered on one side by Front Street and on the other by the promenade. Filled with several varieties of trees, a small duck pond and a dark green, Victorian bandstand, the space afforded both shelter and peace – something Daisy had valued even as a child growing up in the town. A long time spent in prayer and contemplation the previous evening – which had lasted well into the night and involved the shedding of many tears which were probably partly the cause of today's unrelenting headache, those and the usual nightmares anyway – had led Daisy to an idea which she believed might bring the necessary injection of cash and, more importantly, hope into her friend's business. She was planning to talk the idea through with Morag first, and maybe even ask her to put it to Bea as her own suggestion. Daisy didn't care whether she was given credit for the idea, only that her friend was helped out of the black pit of despair into which she had sunk. Daisy herself knew all too well the numbing, crippling effects of depression and, having seen her friend's dull eyes the day before – all light of hope having been extinguished – Daisy was determined to help in one way or another, whether it was welcomed or not.

Opting to walk down Cobble Wynd and across the Town Square to the park, as driving was out of the question in her current state, Daisy hoped fervently that she wouldn't meet anyone chatty en route. The last thing she needed was Mildred Spratt bemoaning her bunions for the umpteenth time. To this end, Daisy wore her biggest winter coat, a relic of her student days. Almost ankle length, the squishy, padded material was more like a duvet than outerwear, complete with a large, fur-lined hood which Daisy currently clasped shut at her chin with her spare hand. This meant that the vicar had tunnel vision, only able to see directly in front of her, and effectively blinkered on both sides by the black fabric which skimmed her cheeks.

All was going well as the vicar gingerly tapped her cane on the slippery, wet cobbles, her pace slow as she navigated the street of small shops, in contrast to her distracted mind which was racing with thoughts of the upcoming conversation with Morag. It wasn't until she felt the cold hardness of the cobbled stones hit her good side with considerable force that Daisy realised she had collided with someone and been, quite literally, knocked off her feet. Too stunned to speak, trying to fight back the sudden urge to cry, Daisy let her hood fall back, grasping around her on the ground for her stick and her backpack, too embarrassed to look up.

"I'm so sorry, vicar. Here, let me help you," Daisy recognised the Irish brogue of Aislin from yesterday. As she tuned into the woman's presence, however, the vicar heard the harsh guffaws of the two men who were with the woman. Unable to speak, Daisy allowed herself to be lifted on both sides – one by the older woman who had spoken and the other by the one named Tallie whom Daisy hadn't yet met properly. To the background jeers and coarse insults of Jugger and Badger, Daisy was hoisted indecorously to her feet, barely able to stand on her own after her fall and so reliant on the two women to keep her upright.

"Tallie! Let me," the voice of Anthony Glendinning came from Daisy's left as the blackness caused by sudden dizziness encroached on her sight, "you shouldn't be lifting in your condition."

"I'm okay," Tallie replied, so quietly Daisy almost didn't hear her despite them being shoulder to shoulder.

"Even so," he replied. Daisy felt her arm being taken by much larger hands as Tallie moved away to let Anthony take her place.

"Yeah, get over here Tallie," Jugger ordered, no humour left in his voice now, "what have I told you about talking to other men, eh? And how does he know about your condition? He the one that knocked you up is he?" Daisy heard the sharp slap of the man's palm against his younger lover's cheek and although she didn't see it, simply felt Anthony's sharp intake of breath, before he let go of the vicar's arm abruptly.

"I haven't laid a hand on Tallie, unlike you!" Anthony roared, "And she's told me what you expect her to do with it, you're not fit to be called a man!"

Slumping on that side now, Daisy moved her left arm to cling to Aislin, so that the older woman held both her shoulders now, though she wasn't paying any attention to Daisy. Shaking her head in disapproval, the Irish woman's eyes were trained on the two men who were now facing off against each other. Turning her head in that direction, gasping at the pain that even that small movement caused her, Daisy saw Tallie, tears running down her face as she tried in vain to hold Jugger back. Anthony Glendinning was up in the man's face, nose to nose, warning him that if he ever touched Tallie again he'd regret it.

"What's going on here?" The high-pitched shriek of Violet Glendinning cut through Daisy's thoughts, though hearing his mother wasn't enough to stop Anthony from taking a swipe at the much bigger bloke.

"Please God, no," Daisy whispered to herself, the plea a literal prayer, as Violet was the last person she wanted to see her in this state. Well, apart from Robert Briggs maybe.

"Anthony! I wondered where you'd disappeared off to, you said you'd carry the shopping," Violet chided, either in complete denial of her son's actions, or simply wishing she could pretend he wasn't now in a wrestling match with Jugger. Either way, the man ignored her completely. Suddenly spotting Daisy, it seemed the vicar gave the woman a cause to take the attention off her wayward offspring. "Reverend! What has happened? Did these awful layabouts assault you? My goodness! Call the police!" She directed the order at Cathy Barnes who had come out from her baker's to see what all the fuss was about, one of a crowd of several folk who were attracted by the ruckus and the hope of a bit of gossip in the usually quiet town.

"Ah, no," Daisy found it hard to form the words, the connection between her brain and her mouth seemed to be malfunctioning. Not that it mattered, as no one was listening to her anyway. Violet was now screeching in Badger's face that he was a criminal and should be locked up, meaning that Aislin had left Daisy to go and try to restore order in that quarter, taking on the tall, willowy local woman in an oral jousting match with accusations of snobbery and prejudice.

Next to them, Tallie was crying hysterically as Anthony and Jugger both had bloodied faces and were now being separated by Billy from the Crow's Nest Inn. When he had appeared, Daisy didn't know, but he was getting up close and personal with Jugger, grabbing the man by the collar of his filthy raincoat and telling the outsider in no uncertain terms that "he and his band of beggars were not welcome" and that "they'd get rid of them one way or the other." Worse still, he seemed to be enjoying the opportunity to voice his strongly held views, practically spitting them forcefully in his adversary's face. Jugger fought to get free of the pub landlord's grasp, eventually settling on butting him in the nose with his forehead and so causing Anthony to jump back into the fight which now involved all three men.

It was a showdown the likes of which Lillymouth had rarely seen. To Daisy, it felt as if all hell had broken loose, and she couldn't help but feel responsible. If she had been looking where she was walking, if she had spoken up at Violet's accusation or preferably earlier, in support of Tallie so that Anthony didn't have to. A panic attack exploded in the vicar's chest then, either without warning or perhaps she had been too distracted to notice the tightening and shallowness of her breath. Her whole body felt like a single ball of pain, and Daisy wondered for a fleeting second if this might really be the end for her. In a muddied, old coat, her face splattered with the same muck, wobbling alone on the side lines, ignored and forgotten, where she had always been. Life had finally defeated the little girl who had wanted nothing more than to be a florist like her grandmother.

Daisy felt her legs give out under her as the blackness that had been threatening her finally took hold. She was aware, as if from a distance, of strong arms grasping her from behind, of sagging gratefully into a hard chest, and of the whispered "I've got you, Daisy," which gave her a moment of blessed reassurance before darkness reigned.

6. YOU OKAY, VICAR?

Daisy was pretty sure she hadn't succumbed to full unconsciousness, as she had the memory of being lifted and quickly transported away from the noise and chaos. She recalled the moment her nose filled with the scent of stargazer lilies, evoking memories from her childhood like a cine reel in her head. She had felt as though she was floating, disconnected from her pain for a few blissful minutes. Until she crashed back down to earth and to the narrow, kind face that was so close to hers.

"Daisy, Daisy come back to me now, you're safe."

It took a moment for the vicar to register her surroundings, though she was not surprised to see who had come to her aid – she had known somehow that it was him even through her strange experience of semi-consciousness.

"You'll have to stop rescuing me like this," Daisy tried to make a joke of it, but the sob that accompanied the last word washed away any chance of humour.

"You know I'm always there if you need me..." he wiped away a tear from just below her right eye with the pad of his thumb – barely making any contact, as if Daisy was made of delicate porcelain – before seemingly shaking himself mentally, his expression becoming one of anger, "Anyway, here, have a sip of water, will you be okay for a moment now that you're awake? I'll lock you in, I just have to..."

"No, don't go out there again Gerald, please, leave it to the police," Daisy knew instinctively that the man would never think of leaving her alone in this particular circumstance unless it were to fight her case in some way, and she couldn't be responsible for more violence.

"I heard they assaulted you Daisy, and I'm afraid that cannot go unpunished."

"No, ah, that isn't what happened, I mean, I don't think it is, I couldn't really see and it all happened so fast. Please don't leave me."

It was her whispered plea that finally got through to Bunch, softening the man's features as he knelt back down beside Daisy where she sat on the small, antique chair behind the counter in his florist shop.

"Okay, ah, okay love, we'll leave that for… ah… the time being. Let's get you checked out, shall we? You're the priority here, not those bast…" It was as if he were telling himself and not her, taking a large breath in to regulate his breathing which had become heavy in his anger.

"No! No hospitals. No doctors. I've had enough of them to last a lifetime," Daisy could feel the tears dripping off her chin now. To be sure, her pain had come back with renewed vigour and if he'd asked her in that moment to name a part of her body that didn't hurt she'd have been hard pushed to do so. Nevertheless, Daisy was adamant, even gripping Bunch's arm to emphasize her point.

"I really think…" he began, only to be interrupted again.

"No. Please Gerald, let's just see how I get on after a hot bath and some painkillers back at the vicarage."

The man didn't look convinced – and if she was
honest, neither was Daisy – but he nodded his
agreement, "Stay here until it's all died down out
there. Let me make you a cup of sweet tea and get you
some pain relief, then when you're feeling stronger I'll
either walk you back home or drive you to the cottage
hospital."

"I have tablets in my bag – emergency rations," Daisy
said, not even wanting to argue that she should leave
right now. Her mind may want her own bath and bed,
but her body protested even the slightest movement.
Besides, she had no desire to have Sylvia fussing over
her like a mother hen, phoning Joe and getting
everyone riled up. Her housekeeper had the best of
intentions, but still…

Unable to manage the stairs into Bunch's flat above the
shop, Daisy had rested where she was on the narrow,
highbacked, mahogany wood chair whilst the man
himself made sure the door was locked and the sign
turned to 'Closed' before going upstairs and returning
with a blanket, a face cloth and a bowl of warm water.
Helping her out of the oversized winter coat, Bunch
then tucked the blanket gently around Daisy's
shivering frame before washing the mud splatters from
her face with a pained expression.

"You could have cuts and bruises that we can't see, broken bones even," he spoke softly as he wiped away the channels her tears had made in the dirt on her cheeks, "please, Daisy."

"A cup of tea and we'll see," Daisy conceded, having realised when she half-stood to take off her coat that she couldn't really balance on her own two feet yet.

This seemed to appease the man and he almost smiled for the first time since their return to the shop, "I'm so sorry I can't make you more comfortable."

"Don't worry, I'm doing fine," Daisy reached out and touched her finger to his cheek, drawn by the concern in Gerald's expression. Their eyes met for a long moment whilst neither spoke. His hand hovered next to her face, the cloth dripping onto Daisy's arm until a loud hammering on the door drew them from their brief but intense connection.

"Reverend Bloom, you in there?" The raised voice of one of the local policemen, Terry Stewart, came loud and clear through the locked door, a moment before the pair saw him peering through the florist's window, craning to see above some tall pampas grass in the display. The man was familiar to Daisy as he had come to church every Sunday since her return, with his wife and two teenagers – the latter rather uncommunicative and surly as young people their age tend to be. They seemed like a lovely family, and Daisy nodded when Bunch asked if she was happy for him to let the man in.

"You okay, Vicar?" The constable asked the moment the door was shut behind him, looking at her, and then to Gerald, and back to Daisy rather pointedly. Given the fact that he had witnessed Bunch's monthly proposals of marriage and resulting rejection – real to everyone in the congregation apart from the vicar and florist themselves – Daisy wasn't surprised that the man was rather shocked to find the two of them alone here.

"Yes, ah, just needed a moment to catch my breath, Constable," Daisy managed a watery smile, which she hoped hadn't looked more like a grimace. The side of her face which had made contact with the pavement was really throbbing now, "Mr. Bunch was kind enough to let me rest here."

"Oh!" Frown lines appeared in the man's forehead as if he couldn't understand how that could be the case, or in what turn of events the vicar would ever allow it to happen. Clearly employing the diplomacy required in his profession, though, despite having an obvious personal wish to know exact details, he simply said, "Ah well, I do need to ask you a few questions Reverend Daisy, if you're up to it?"

"I can leave if you like," Gerald said, looking directly at Daisy, though he made no sign of movement.

"No, please stay, and yes officer, let's just get it over with."

As Daisy confirmed that no, she did not think she had been assaulted, that yes, she believed the men involved in the fracas were equally at fault and she didn't want to name any one person as the main aggressor, and that no she didn't wish to press any charges, her frayed nerves reacted to reliving the event and she found herself once again weeping profusely. A fact that embarrassed the vicar even more than her dishevelled appearance and, what she considered to be, all the unnecessary attention.

"I think that's probably all the vicar can manage for now," Bunch said, seeing Daisy's renewed distress and only at the last minute remembering to affect the loud, obnoxious voice that was part of his public persona.

"I'll take you home, Vicar," the policeman said, eying the other man distastefully.

"Oh, ah, that's very kind, but I have Joe Pierce coming to collect me," it was a small white lie, and Daisy didn't even know why the words had come out of her mouth. Maybe she had a concussion after all? But she found herself wanting to stay with Bunch for a while longer and to have that cup of tea he had promised.

Not looking convinced about leaving her alone with her would-be suitor, Terry Stewart said nothing for a moment, drawing his eyebrows together and pursing his lips tightly as if the whole thing represented a great conundrum, until at length, when the silence had become decidedly awkward, he said, "Right then," and saw himself quickly out.

7. HER DIRTY LITTLE SECRET

Daisy and Gerald looked at each other in silence once the police officer had left. She could feel her cheeks heating even underneath the new bruises which she knew must be there and prayed he wouldn't ask her why she had lied in order to spend more time together. Daisy herself didn't even have the answer to that one.

She needn't have worried, however, as Bunch proceeded as if the interruption had not occurred, picking up the now-cold bowl of water and face cloth, and smiling gently, "I'll get us that tea, Daisy."

The vicar was thankful for a few minutes to pull herself together. She hoisted her backpack onto her lap, trying to ignore the shooting pain down her side as she did so, and rummaged inside for the strong painkillers she kept as an emergency stash for when she was out and about and it became too much. She wasn't a woman prone to studying her reflection – indeed, Daisy often didn't even look in the mirror on a morning, simply brushed and plaited her hair while sitting on her bed and called it done. Now, though, she found herself pulling out the tiny flip-open mirror that had been in the inside pocket of her bag for so long she couldn't remember why she had put it there in the first place. Certainly, Daisy never had any make-up to check or reapply. Removing the old, furry Murray mint that was stuck to the metal case and flipping it open, the vicar cautiously raised the mirror to her face, feeling a disproportionate amount of trepidation for what she would see there.

"Blummin' heck!" Daisy snapped the case shut and shoved the offending article back in her bag. Between the swollen, bloodshot eyes, the remaining streaks of dirt that Gerald hadn't scrubbed hard enough to remove, and the bruises that were blooming on her injured cheek, she was an absolute mess. Her blonde hair was plastered to her forehead, and the rest seemed to have escaped the confines of her braid. Daisy tried to run her fingers through the knotted rats tails, only to discover her hair bobble was missing from the bottom, "Well, that explains that," she whispered to herself. Normally not giving a care what she looked like – as Daisy believed the way she treated people was what they would remember anyway, not whether she was dressed to the nines and her face made up to match – she had to admit to feeling despondent at the thought that Bunch had seen her in this state.

"Why do I even care how he sees me?" Daisy snapped at herself, louder this time.

"How who sees you?" Gerald asked, emerging through the side door with a tray holding a teapot and two mugs.

"Oh! Just returning a text," Daisy lied, wondering why the truth was suddenly no longer her ally.

Gerald looked slightly confused, since she didn't even have her phone out, but thankfully said no more on the matter and proceeded to pour the tea, even producing a couple of chocolate bars from his pocket. "I thought we could do with the sugar hit," he grinned and Daisy happily accepted the snack.

"So the nightmares only began again when you

returned to Lillymouth?" Gerald asked. It was the first thing he had said for the past ten minutes, having simply listened quietly as Daisy explained the reasons for her current tiredness whilst they both sipped their tea.

Why she had confided in him about the unrelenting flashbacks to the time around her Gran's murder that only ever came back to her in dream form, the vicar had no idea, as she certainly hadn't felt compelled to share with anyone else. Up until now, they had felt like her dirty little secret. Residual shame and guilt from that time seeping through her unconscious into her current frame of mind – that she and Gran hadn't been in a good place with each other and had been arguing a lot, that she had gone out with Bea and her mum on a shopping spree the afternoon of Gran's death, that she hadn't stuck around to clear her own name when the police decided not to press charges, turning her back on those who loved her... the list went on and on.

"Yes, I mean, I had them for years at first, well into my early twenties, but their reappearance has only been since I came back here."

"Well, and I mean I'm no expert, but maybe it would help to look around this place when you feel better? The shop's tiny of course, but you could look in the basement room and up in the flat in case that might trigger any memories to help you unravel everything? Or even just to get some closure, whatever that might be?"

"Um…That's very kind, Gerald, I might take you up on that," she deliberately left her answer vague. Daisy was grateful for the offer, though her immediate instinct was to shun the idea and protect what little peace of mind she had left. After all, the more she let her past experiences in, the more they seemed to be dominating her thoughts nowadays. She certainly wasn't sure if she should actively seek those long-forgotten memories out. But she did want to find Gran's killer…

"Whenever you want," Gerald said, setting down his cup, "now, those painkillers have had a chance to work, let's see if you can stand up."

When Daisy finally got back to the vicarage – with Bunch's help after using the last of her energy persuading him she didn't need medical attention, though he left her at the door before Sylvia spotted him and started asking questions – it was to find out that in all the hubbub of that morning she had completely forgotten to let Morag know she wasn't going to be able to meet up in the park. Bea's mum had, in fact, come looking for her at the vicarage when Daisy didn't answer her calls, thinking that there must be something wrong. The guilt that sprang up on hearing this news, coupled with Sylvia's aghast look of concern as she imparted it whilst staring openly at Daisy's injured face, was enough to make the vicar wish she had stayed in the sanctuary of the florist's shop.

"So, ah, you'd perhaps better phone the woman," Sylvia concluded, stroking the pointy ears of her lap rabbit, Malone. The hulking white creature stared at Daisy, who had collapsed on the opposite sofa the moment she came in, as if she were a very unwelcome interruption to the afternoon's cosy TV viewing.

"I will, of course," Daisy wished she hadn't sat down, as now she had the impending discomfort of having to haul herself back up and off to her bedroom to lie down.

"Can I get you anything, Vicar?" Sylvia asked, frowning at the state of Daisy's black skirt which had evidently just caught her eye. Daisy had so far kept her explanation of the morning's events especially brief, but no doubt Sylvia would hear every detail – both true and embellished – on the town's social media grapevine by this evening anyway. The vicar appreciated the sentiment, since normally nothing short of a bomb scare would be allowed to disturb the afternoon reruns of 'Diagnosis Murder,' yet here her housekeeper was offering assistance and it wasn't even an ad break.

"No, no, thank you, I think I'll have a nap and then a long soak in the bath," *And a double shot of whisky for good measure,* Daisy thought, but kept her planned afternoon drinking to herself.

The fog in her brain was too thick to navigate as Daisy lay down to sleep, stripping off her muddy clothes and snuggling under the blankets in her underwear. She didn't even try to process what had happened that day, nor to contemplate what implications it may have. It was all too difficult for her throbbing head and the migraine which had come back full force now that the adrenaline from her accident had worn off. Even Jacob eyed her suspiciously from the comfy chair in the corner, giving the vicar a wide birth and merely swiping a paw to knock her Bible off the armrest to indicate his displeasure at having not been given the attentive greeting he was due.

Daisy left the Good Book where it lay, thinking that God would surely understand that she had reached her limits right now. She was just human after all.

8. NEITHER BRIGHT, NOR BEAUTIFUL

It wasn't until the Sunday service that the vicar was seen in public again that week. Daisy had been holed up in her room, batting off Sylvia's attempts to mother her, and shooing the cat out at what felt like thirty minute intervals. Whenever Daisy left her room to go to the bathroom or the kitchen, the furtive feline would sneak back in and the vicar would return to find him ensconced in her spot on her pillow or curled up on her laptop. Shunning company, and having emailed the Bishop with renewed vigour asking when a curate might be available to lighten her load within the parish, Daisy had performed her duties via online Zoom meetings and electronic messages for the remainder of the week.

Even by Sunday, her body was still feeling as though it had been three rounds in the ring with Muhammad Ali, and Daisy had to drag herself the short distance across to the church building, her sour mood not helped by the screeching sounds of the organ as she entered the main chapel. Before Christmas, Daisy had – with much tact and diplomacy, she thought – offered the parish's only organist, Mildred Spratt, the opportunity to take a few lessons from her counterpart in the next town over.

"Just to expand your range of Christmas carols," Daisy had quickly added on seeing the thunderous expression on the face of the tiny, sparrow-like woman.

"Do you have a problem with my current repertoire, Vicar?" Had been the curt response.

Daisy wasn't sure how to tell the organist that every hymn sounded like 'All Things Bright and Beautiful' or that she made the melodic instrument sound like a couple of cats fighting in the back alley. So, she backtracked quickly, placating the woman by explaining how she herself was tone deaf. She wasn't, of course, and now had the weekly reminder of that decision to appease blasted loudly throughout what should be a place of sanctuary, cursing herself for her visceral dislike of confrontation.

Thankfully, Daisy's mood was lifted later when she stepped onto the pulpit and cast her eyes around those assembled. There, after an absence of a few months from the Sunday service and in her usual spot on the second row was Bea, sitting with Andrew and her mum, little Daisy Mae on her lap. Daisy smiled at her friend, only to receive a blank stare in return. Nevertheless, it was a step forward and Daisy was grateful. She assumed Morag had spoken with her daughter and managed to get Bea out of the house for a while. Daisy made a mental note to speak to the family after the service and to try once again to rebuild bridges. Perhaps even get little Daisy Mae booked in for her Christening service – after all, what could bring more joy?

Another notable member of the morning's congregation was the young woman, Tallie, from the group of activists. She sat with Anthony Glendinning, near the back of the church and about eight pews removed from his parents. Her appearance surprised the vicar, though Daisy did not show it. In fact, she sent a beaming smile the girl's way and received a small, nervous one in return. Whilst everyone was welcome in the Lord's house, Daisy was admittedly glad that the rest of the activists' group hadn't joined them. Tensions were running high, and according to the social media posts Sylvia had shown her with glee, some of the townsfolk were advocating the formation of a mob to run the unwelcome visitors out of town. The vicar certainly didn't want to be refereeing any kind of confrontation, especially after what had happened earlier that week. As far as she knew from Sylvia's admittedly unreliable informants, no charges had been pressed against either Jugger or the two local men, and Daisy hoped they had all learned their lesson and would pursue more peaceful methods of conflict resolution in future. Somehow, though, she doubted it.

Whilst a message on tolerance and acceptance might therefore have been more fitting, Daisy had chosen to speak about perseverance and resilience for the sermon that day. Partly because the theme spoke to her own current frame of mind, and also because it meant she could recycle a sermon she had written for her previous parish and which the townsfolk of Lillymouth hadn't heard from her before. This had freed up some of her time in the second half of the week, allowing the vicar more opportunity to rest and recuperate.

A large bunch of flowers had appeared on the vicarage doorstep the previous day, with a card that read simply, 'Wishing you happy dreams,' and Daisy had known immediately who it was from, hiding her large smile from her housekeeper. Of course, it didn't take a genius to work out the giver of the gift, since the man in question was the only florist in town. Sylvia had been very vocal that the "creepy letch should leave the poor vicar alone," and had offered to speak to the man and tell him "in no uncertain terms to back the heck off." Even now, from her position up front during the first hymn, Daisy could see the woman giving Bunch her best look of disapproval. The florist himself seemed undeterred by this, however, and deliberately sent a lascivious wink in the vicar's direction when he saw Sylvia watching. Daisy tried her best not to react and stifled her amusement, though she realised in that moment that Gerald Bunch had been the source of her only moments of levity that whole week.

Things were very much neither bright, nor beautiful at the end of the service, despite the clanking chords which purported otherwise, as Daisy found herself completely shunned by Bea who chose to slip out of the chapel by the side door with the baby during the last hymn, presumably so she did not have to face the vicar whilst exiting the church at the main door with the rest of the congregation. Daisy swallowed down the hurt, plastered a smile on her face and a few minutes later tried not to cry when Morag told her that

Bea needed more time and would hopefully come around eventually, but that there was no need for Christening arrangements as Bea had already had her daughter baptised in the church at the next town over. As the tiny girl's godmother – or not, as it would now appear – Daisy was extremely hurt by this and had to force herself to speak past the huge lump in her throat. Nevertheless, the vicar invited Morag round for coffee at the vicarage during the week to discuss the idea she'd had for income for the bookshop, and then politeness dictated she turn to greet the next person queuing to leave. It had been far from the encounter she'd hoped for.

With relief, Daisy saw that it was Gerald who was in line to share some pleasantries next, and she mustered up the best smile she could manage. Apparently the attempt was woefully inadequate, however, as the man's expression changed immediately upon having a closer look at the vicar's face and he whispered, "Daisy, what's happened? Something new?" whilst aloud he all but shouted, "A bunch of blooms! You still not ready yet?" so as to keep up the charade.

"I'll tell you later, maybe I could make that visit to your shop tomorrow morning?" Daisy whispered, adding loudly, "What an impertinent man!"

"Impertinent indeed," Violet Glendinning snapped from behind, and Gerald made a reluctant exit.

"Violet, good morning, and Percy, how are you both today?" Daisy asked, affecting her most insincere voice. Violet wore a bright red, knitted beret, adorned with some kind of red bird feathers, and sunglasses with matching red frames which looked out of place on this freezing morning in February. Ridiculous even. Daisy knew her judgement was harsh – especially made on a parishioner's appearance – but given the woman's attitude, she allowed herself to indulge mentally in some less-than-ecclesiastical thoughts.

"Well, how do you think we are? After our Anthony was dragged into the police station this week and given a formal warning of all things. And you were there, Vicar, the cause of the whole debacle, you should have spoken up before it all got to that point..."

"Now dear..." Percy interrupted, though if looks could kill the glare his wife turned on him then would have had the man laid out cold. Instead, he stopped short after only those two words and sauntered off.

"Well, your Anthony seemed very cosy with one of the activists at the back of the church just then," Daisy bit back, unable to help herself, "so he's clearly making his own choices to hang around with them." Judging by the dawning horror on the face of the woman opposite, Violet hadn't seen the pair enter the back of the church after her.

"Something must be done!" Violet shrieked, causing a few heads to turn in the groups of people milling around chatting on the grass outside the chapel doors as she hurried off after her husband, no doubt to chew his ear off about the whole thing.

"With you, definitely," Daisy muttered to herself, thankful that everyone else seemed to have filed out in the meantime and there were no more hands left to shake or polite chit chat to be engaged in.

With a sigh of relief, the vicar stepped back inside the cold church foyer, shutting the heavy doors behind her. It wasn't until she walked back into the main chapel itself, deep in her own thoughts, that Daisy realised she wasn't alone.

9. OUT OF THE FRYING PAN, INTO THE FIRE

"Anthony, Tallie, I thought everyone had left," Daisy said, stopping short at the end of the pew on which the two sat. Violet Glendinning's son was a tall, broad man who, Daisy knew from Sylvia's intel, had completed at least three university degrees, interspersed with several trips backpacking around the world. She guessed that made him about her own age, though he hadn't attended the local school with her so Daisy couldn't be sure. Anthony must be intelligent though, the vicar thought, but not inclined to use his education to find a stable job which meant he was still living at home with his parents when back in the town. His shaggy appearance and general unkempt look gave the man the air of someone younger, though perhaps not young enough to be holding hands with a petite woman who couldn't be out of her teens.

Daisy smiled, whilst trying to mentally remove her judgemental cap that seemed to have become stuck on that morning.

"Vicar, we are in need of your professional assistance," Anthony said, beaming at her with the confidence of a certain ginger cat who got the cream. His accent had none of the Yorkshire twang that was prevalent in the town.

"And what help would that be?" Daisy asked, slipping onto the bench beside Tallie and resting her cane next to her. She smiled at the girl, and received a nervous glance back. *Hmm*, Daisy thought to herself.

"How quickly can you perform a marriage?" Anthony asked, lifting his hand which was joined with Tallie's, as if that would be all the explanation required.

Daisy hid her shock behind a mask of professional efficiency, "Well, there is generally some pre-marital counselling, the reading of the banns... ah, finding a date, the marriage licence of course..."

"No, no, I mean if it were a tiny affair, just us and

whatever witnesses are legally required. If I got an emergency licence or whatnot... I don't know all the terminology vicar, but you get my drift."

"I do, yes," Daisy said, turning her full attention to the young woman next to her who had yet to say a word, "Tallie, isn't it? We haven't been properly introduced. How are you doing?"

"I, um, I," Tallie looked to the vicar, then to Anthony, who replied on her behalf.

"She's very excited, and keen to get it done as fast as me," Anthony answered.

"I see," Daisy replied slowly, her gut telling her she needed to tread carefully and quickly with this. Something didn't sit right with her, "well, there is much to be discussed. Perhaps having those conversations with you both separately would be best..."

When she saw Anthony about to interrupt again, no doubt with reiterations of their pressing timeframe, Daisy added, "That is my preferred way of doing things, however big or small the ceremony you're after," another small white lie, "Tallie, why don't you come back for some lunch at the vicarage and we can discuss it there. Anthony, I could meet you tomorrow evening, perhaps at The Crow's Nest? I'm afraid I already have a lot in my diary for the coming days."

The man was clearly not happy with this arrangement, but Daisy squared her shoulders and gave off the air that she would brook no further argument if they wanted her help in the matter.

"Fine, off you go Tals, I'll see you later," it was said through gritted teeth and accompanied by a small slap on the young woman's bottom as she stood. Daisy pretended not to notice the intimacy and certainly didn't care that she might have put the man's nose out of joint. She had the chance to talk to Tallie alone, and that was the most important concern right now.

When Sylvia saw the two women enter the vicarage kitchen she quickly whipped the house rabbit off the table, where he seemed to have been tucking into an almighty salad of leafy greens. Next to him, Jacob refused to be budged as he was wolfing down what looked like a portion of the fish pie that Daisy knew was for Sunday lunch. It seemed her housekeeper did have a soft spot for the cat's appetite after all!

"I've just brought Tallie back for lunch," Daisy said by way of explanation, though it was already evident.

Sylvia blushed and quickly removed the two animals' plates, to the extreme displeasure of the greedy tom cat, who yowled and swatted the table with his paw ineffectually. Giving his rotund rear a small shove to encourage the animal off the surface they were about to put their own plates on, Daisy turned to the young woman still hovering in the doorway. Tallie looked white, her eyes huge and round in her gaunt face.

"Come and sit down, lass," Sylvia said gently, indicating a chair, "we don't stand on ceremony here."

"I, ah, it's quite a while since I've had a meal in an actual house. I mean, in someone's home," the young woman said, her lower lip trembling for a brief second before she appeared to bring her emotions back under control.

"Well, it's nothing fancy, just fish pie and veg," Sylvia said, dishing three huge portions onto plates.

"It smells delicious, thank you," Tallie said. The young woman was very softly spoken and no sooner had her bottom touched the seat than a high-pitched sound of police sirens filled the air. Tallie shot back up with a small shriek, her eyes alert and focused on the large kitchen window.

"It's just Archie, the mynah bird," Daisy said, as if this

was a completely normal occurrence – which of course, in the vicarage it was. She chastised the bird and encouraged their visitor to sit back down, but not before noticing the effect the potential arrival of the local constabulary had had on the young woman. Tallie's hand was shaking as she accepted the cutlery and plate which Sylvia handed her, and her jaw rigid with suppressed fear. Smiling, Daisy didn't acknowledge the evident anxiety, instead starting a conversation about the time of year, the bulbs that would soon be sprouting into blooms in the vicarage garden, and the chance of snow before that happened. It was the usual typically British, inconsequential chat preferred at social gatherings and seemed to put their visitor at ease.

If either Daisy or Sylvia were shocked at the speed at which the young woman cleared her plate, ate seconds and then demolished a bowl of apple crumble and custard, neither said as much. Quite the opposite – the housekeeper, in particular, seemed gratified that their guest had enjoyed her food, and blushed when Tallie commented on how tasty it was.

When the meal was cleared away, and Sylvia had refused their offers of help, Daisy and Tallie took two large mugs of hot tea into the sitting room. No sooner had they both placed the steaming cups onto the coffee table and sat down on opposite sofas, than Daisy was knocked backwards by a giant, orange ball of fluff jumping onto her lap. Tallie didn't get off scot-free either, since the oversized house rabbit apparently wasn't picky about whether it was Sylvia in her usual seat by the fire, or a complete stranger. All he needed was a cosy lap to settle down on for his afternoon nap.

"I'm so sorry," Daisy said, about to shoo the animal off Tallie.

"No, no, leave him, he's okay," the young woman said, stroking the white fur gently whilst the rabbit himself gave the vicar a look of haughty smugness.

"So," Daisy began softly, "you want to marry Anthony, do you?" It was deliberately phrased as a question rather than a statement, and the vicar let the pause lengthen as she waited for a reply.

"I, well, I, he seems lovely and it would, ah, solve some problems for me," Tallie answered eventually.

The evasive response was not lost on Daisy, who nodded and continued, "You know, my Gran would often talk about going 'out of the frying pan into the fire' and I wonder if that might be an appropriate phrase for your situation?"

Again a lengthy silence, as the young woman opposite ran her hands up the rabbit's long ears, looking anywhere but at the vicar. This time, however, an answer wasn't forthcoming, so Daisy pressed on, "Tell me how you and Anthony met."

"Well, ah, we were at a festival down south – the four of us, I mean. Aislin doesn't really like all that loud music and drug taking, but Jugger was meeting up with a contact, so ah, there we were and I met Anthony in a beer tent. Jugger had got me a job serving pints for a bit of cash," It was the most Daisy had ever heard the woman say.

"And you hit it off?" The vicar prompted.

"Yes, well, I mean he was pretty drunk and was on his way back from Malaysia or somewhere so jet lagged too, but he invited me to come up here and visit him in Lillymouth."

"And the invitation was for all four of you?" Daisy asked, surprised that that would be the case.

"Oh, well, ah I doubt it, but of course Jugger wouldn't let me leave with Anthony. Downright refused at first, but then he asked me for the town name and when he'd done a bit of digging online he said it would be a good jaunt for all of us. Complete change of heart."

"So, nothing to do with the new train engine at all then?" Daisy was confused.

"Oh! I, ah, I mean it must be a news article on those plans that Jugger had seen, mustn't it?" Tallie fidgeted with the heavy metal hoop in her right ear.

Daisy was pretty sure nothing had been announced in the press yet, given everything was still in the planning stages and they'd only had confirmation of the lottery funding two days before the supposed activists had arrived. She didn't mention this, however, instead saying, "Do you move around a lot then? Which environmental concerns are you particularly passionate about?"

Tallie looked at her blankly, giving the impression of a deer caught in the headlights. Daisy took pity on her and changed the direction of the conversation, storing the information up to ponder on later.

"So, you won't know this, but in my previous life I used to work with victims of violence," Daisy began cautiously – if anything would cause her guest to leave it would be this, "and I heard the slap Jugger gave you when I was knocked over. That alone would give you good cause to leave the man immediately and without a backward glance, you don't need to have another man rescue you. You and your unborn baby. You are pregnant, aren't you, Tallie? I heard the end of the argument you had when I was at the train station the other day and then Anthony's comment about your 'condition.' There are plenty of people here who would help you, right here in the vicarage we have a spare bedroom that you could use in the meantime…"

The young woman opposite her looked shocked, then angry, and jumped up to leave, completely disregarding the animal on her knee, before pausing after a couple of steps as if the choice was warring inside her. Daisy struggled to her feet, using the armrest for leverage and held out a conciliatory hand, "Tallie, let me help you."

"You can't protect me from him! No one can, except maybe Anthony and his family. I don't know. I don't have any options. I have nowhere to go. Anthony has been kind with me. I just…" her fists were clenched by her sides, her eyes glassy with the tears she refused to let fall.

Daisy closed the distance between them and hugged the younger woman to her.

"There are always options Tallie. Don't rush into marriage or even another relationship. Let me help you, I have strong connections with a women's refuge in Leeds. I could take you there…"

"Maybe," Tallie pulled away and darted then for the door to the hallway. Daisy let her go this time, a sadness enveloping her.

One thing the vicar knew for sure, she wouldn't be marrying this scared young woman to Anthony Glendinning, or any other man for that matter. Though she certainly wasn't going to give up on helping her.

10. THE SPIDER AND THE FLY

"I didn't want to mention it yesterday, as you seemed to have enough on your mind with that nice girl, but ah, Rosemary Wessex from the library told me after the church service that she'd seen your Uncle Joe having it out with one of the activists – the big, brutish one – down by the pier the other night. Lots of shouting, apparently, about you having been assaulted…" Sylvia trailed off when she saw the black look on Daisy's face.

One quiet cup of coffee before an extremely hectic day, is that too much to ask? Daisy thought, *Without more bad news and drama?*

Aloud she replied, "Oh my goodness! I spoke to him on the phone after the accident and told him I was okay. Persuaded him not to come over here fussing, or to storm off to the station… or so I thought."

"Aye well, apparently Rosemary thinks she and the other ladies from the book club may have inadvertently stoked some fires there, as they hold the group in The Boatyard once a month, and on Friday evening there had been some discussion about your, ah, incident in the street."

"What?" Daisy could feel the heat rising under her dog collar, "I thought they discussed books not local gossip?"

"Well, ah, you know what these get togethers can be like," Sylvia said sheepishly, knowing full well she would've been there too had she not been full of cold at the end of last week.

"Right, well, I'll have to fit in a visit to Joe between my calls today," Daisy gulped down the last of her drink in annoyance, "and maybe a call to the library!"

Sylvia had the grace to look bad about the whole thing, though even in her anger Daisy knew that none of it was her housekeeper's fault. She gave the woman a quick pat on the shoulder to reassure her that everything was okay, and then stomped out of the kitchen, ignoring the shrieks of the mynah bird in the hallway, who was inclined to tell her "It's all a stitch

77

up!"

Thankfully, the first on her list was a visit to the florist's and Daisy's mood was much improved on the short walk over there, looking forward as she was to talking everything through with her friend. On arrival, however, it was clear Bunch was quite out of sorts – decidedly so, in fact, and in a much darker mood than Daisy had ever seen him. Whilst physically, the man's appearance had had what one might call a 'glow up' – gone were the straggly hairs on his chin, the old-fashioned, wire rimmed spectacles and the greased down centre parting – mentally, he seemed at an all-time low.

"Gerald, is everything okay?" Daisy asked gently, after having had to hammer on the shop door to attract the man's attention, when normally the florist's would be open very early on Mondays for flower deliveries. Eventually emerging from the small staircase that Daisy knew led to the basement room, Bunch opened the door with barely a nod in the vicar's direction, bent his tall frame to pick up the boxes of fresh cuts that had been dumped on the doorstep, and indicated that she should follow him inside where he promptly locked the front door again.

"Ah, well, no, not so much," was the curt reply, "I think it's time I told you the truth, Daisy. I could do with a confidante to be honest, and then of course I want to hear all about why you were upset at the morning service yesterday." He descended back into the bowels of the building and Daisy followed, careful not to trip on her cane as she navigated the narrow, uneven stairway.

"Of course, you have always lent an ear to my woes, Gerald, of course, I'll..." the vicar stopped short as they entered the space. In her grandmother's time, this cool basement room had been perfect for the storage of fresh flowers until they were needed for weekend weddings and suchlike. There had been a high table, just the right height for preparing the bouquets, a set of shelves filled with ribbons and laces of all different widths and colours, and a cosy settee for when they needed a break and a cuppa. Now, however, the room had been stripped bare. Even down to the brick on the far wall, where a piece of plyboard seemed to cover an almighty hole which stretched almost the full height and width of that side. The rest of the room still had its plaster painted in the pastel lilac Gran had chosen, but it looked like damp was rising, and with it not a little mould, no doubt caused by the gaping cavity.

Daisy couldn't help the gasp which escaped as her

hand flew to her mouth in shock.

"Sorry, I should've warned you, mind your step there, I haven't cleared out all the rubble yet," Gerald said, on a monotone, as if this were the most ordinary scene in the world.

"Y-yes, I can see," was all Daisy could manage.

"I guess you're wondering what on earth I've been doing?" Gerald said.

"Um, I haven't quite got that far yet," Daisy replied, "I'm just, ah, taking it all in to be honest."

"Quite. Well, as you can see, I've been digging. For a long time, since I bought the place from you, in fact."

"But why?" Daisy was at a loss.

"Okay," he took a deep breath, "I know this will sound crazy. I am – was – an assistant professor of archaeology at a university down south. But my biggest passion was always treasure hunting. Ever since I was a boy, raised by my uncle in one of those old, haunted houses you see in black and white films from decades ago, I've been quite, well, obsessed you would say. One day in my mid-twenties I was researching a paper I was writing on the Yorkshire smugglers of the nineteenth century, and I found an old map stuck under the back cover of the dusty tome I'd found in the local archives over in Whitby."

"Let me guess, a map of Lillymouth," Daisy interjected, having been told all the old smugglers' tales by Uncle Joe as a girl.

"Indeed. And not just any map. One that showed the secret tunnels that run from the caves at the far end of the beach right under the town. Somewhere in those tunnels, there's supposed to be a haul of treasure that was never discovered."

"I've heard the stories of Smugglers' Isle, but nothing about tunnels," Daisy was intrigued now.

"Well, they caught my interest, more than that really, they began to dominate my thoughts, and I made some visits to the town and the caves but couldn't find any entrance from that end. Especially reliant as I was on tides and weather conditions, and wanting to keep my actions under wraps so to speak. So, I studied the maps more closely and worked out where one of the tunnels seemed to end…" He looked at Daisy expectantly, as if she would automatically put two and two together. As it was, the vicar's brain was whirring as fast as it could and still couldn't quite keep up with all the new information, so Bunch spelt it out for her, "right under this shop."

"Oh! So that's why you were determined to have it,"
Daisy whispered, "Even paying far more than the
guide price." *Did he kill my Gran for it?* Was Daisy's first
thought as her breathing began to come in short, sharp
gasps and her head started to feel like it was full of
candy floss.

"Daisy, the conditions aren't good for breathing down
here... so much dust... should've thought, so sorry,
caught up in my own brain this morning..." Gerald
grabbed her by the elbow and hurried Daisy back up to
the main shop and onto the chair behind the counter.

Daisy took a moment to collect herself, while Gerald
poured her a glass of water from the jug on the shelf
behind them and knelt down beside her, gazing
anxiously up into her face.

"Would you have got the shop... at any cost?" Daisy
whispered, feeling sick to her stomach that she was
potentially sitting so close to her grandmother's killer.
She was determined not to cry, but her eyes didn't
seem to get the message.

"Well, ah, there's a right time for everything, Daisy
and it was the right time for me to follow my dream. I
had some inheritance, and... Oh! If you mean, would I
have killed for it? Then of course not! I'm not a
murderer!" His voice rose slightly and the man seemed

offended, standing quickly and turning his back on the vicar as he spoke.

"That's rubbish!" Daisy replied, causing the man opposite to spin around quickly, his eyes wide in shock, "Not about you being a murderer, Gerald, at least I hope not, I mean about the right time for things. It certainly wasn't the right time for Gran to die!" Daisy's own voice was loud and high pitched now, and she clamped her mouth shut, not wanting to sound like Violet Glendinning. They were getting some strange looks through the glass fronted shop window anyway. No doubt this would lead to more gossip about the couple, but right now Daisy didn't care.

Bunch took a deep breath and apologised, "I'm sorry, love, this wasn't how I wanted this conversation to go. Will you come upstairs to the flat and we can talk it through over a cuppa? I should've suggested that in the first place…" he ran his long fingers through his now-fluffy hair and Daisy felt a moment of pity for the man, not flinching as he reached forward and used those same fingers to gently wipe the tears from her cheek.

Perhaps against her better judgement, the vicar found herself following the florist upstairs, hoping she wasn't about to be the fly to his spider.

11. THE GOLD RUSH DAYS

"Can I start again?" Bunch asked when they were settled on his pristine black leather sofa in his immaculate and somewhat sterile lounge. The open plan kitchen and sitting room had been decorated in bright white since Daisy had lived there – no longer the floral chintz and cosy homeliness, not that she had really expected it to be – and didn't even look like the same space, "I invited you to help with the nightmares, not add to them, Daisy, I'm so sorry."

"It's okay, I just... it was a shock. So much to take in at once," Daisy ventured cautiously, "you seemed very out of sorts when I arrived. Was it to do with... with the tunnels?"

"It was, but let me start at the beginning again. To put

your mind at ease. I saw the maps, I figured out the approximate layout of the tunnels, I bought the shop under my deceased uncle's name so as to remain off the radar so to speak. Treasure hunting is big business, Daisy, it's like an underground society and I am already searchable on the Internet under my real name for my earlier efforts and as an archaeologist. I wanted to remain incognito. If certain people found out I was here, it would be like moths to a flame."

"I see, it is quite literally an underground society for you, then, what with all the digging," Daisy attempted to make a joke but it fell flat.

"What? Oh yes, I see, yes indeed. Anyway, I'm allergic to animals so I found the spot where the rats got into the basement here…"

"Yes, Gran and I could never quite stop them, always had traps out. Couldn't understand where they came from, guess I know now."

"Yes, my ridiculous sneezing led me to the correct wall, and then to the tunnel opening. Over the years I've managed to shore up and clear a safe path all the way to the beach caves."

"No! My goodness, Gerald, that has to be a couple of miles at least!"

"Well, it has been fifteen years since I began, and I can only really work at night though the tunnels were already there, I was just re-opening them so to speak… but about this whole Gerald thing. I like you Daisy," he grasped his hands tightly and twisted them, a sign of anxiety Daisy was all-too familiar with, "I want to be completely honest with you, my real name is Marcus, Marcus Caldwell. But if we could keep that between the two of us… Bunch is better for a florist, after all," he gave a feeble wink and Daisy smiled, appeased by the admission.

"Well, Marcus, truth is very important to me, so thank you. And yes, I will keep your secret, as long as you're doing nothing illegal. But what about whatever has you so out of sorts?"

"Ah yes, well, last night I made my way to the caves, checking my maps again for where I should start digging into offshoots from the main tunnels, as that's where the treasure is likely to be, somewhere off the main route. It's backbreaking, as I can't stand up in them fully and… anyway, I digress, I was about to emerge into the main cave when I heard voices so I held back, in the dark shadows right in the depths, listening."

"And who was it?" Daisy was intrigued now. *Could it*

be Uncle Joe? Does he know about the tunnels?

"Those supposed activists!" Marcus almost shouted in his indignance, "The newcomers, right in the cave, near the tunnel entrance at the back! That spot is so hidden, so secret, that I don't think the locals even know about it. Certainly, I've not seen anyone there at night in all these years, only a few families playing about just inside the cave entrance during the day.

"Maybe they were hiding in there to take drugs?" *Or worse,* Daisy tried not to let her mind wander.

"Well, I'd like to think so, but the big one, Jugger is it? Well, he said "it must be around here" as if he had some kind of inside knowledge and they were searching for the tunnel entrance. Of course, I waited, in the cold darkness while they stomped around with flashlights, the other three moaning, until they finally gave up, the younger girl complaining that she was cold. But it's got me rattled Daisy. Is it a race to the finish line now that I've put in all the hard work? When I first reached that cave from my tunnel going from here, it was so blocked up I had to batter my way through. I wish I'd left it sealed now. Don't know why I didn't... perhaps I should go down tonight and shore it back up..." he was lost in thought and Daisy got the impression she was invisible now.

"Have you ever, ah, actually, found any? Treasure?" Daisy asked, wondering if the man was actually mentally stable and not creating a world of his own making.

"Some small pieces of gold jewellery, yes, buried in the mud of the tunnel floor. Obviously dropped over a century ago from the main haul," the man jumped up abruptly and disappeared into what Daisy knew was one of two small bedrooms in the apartment, re-emerging a couple of minutes later with a parcel made from a cotton handkerchief tied with florists' string. Unwrapping it delicately, he produced two chains and a pendant, as well as a small brooch. To be honest, they weren't much to look at, but Daisy imagined it must be a bit like the gold fever of the gold rush days – when you found a grain it spurred you on to continue.

"So you feel under a certain time pressure now," Daisy said as she gently held the antique pieces.

"I do, and I'd like to know how those thieves found out about…" the man clamped his mouth shut then and took a deep breath, "Anyway, Daisy, enough about me, I hope you don't think I'm mad. Tell me about yesterday, and these bad dreams."

By the time the vicar had recounted the news of Daisy Mae already being christened and then had another look around all three floors of the building – hoping that by seeing there were few resemblances left to how the place used to be, she would stop reliving the arguments and memories of the day she found her gran's body – it was lunchtime and the vicar had to rush out to visit the elderly parishioners on her list. She refrained from mentioning Tallie's visit to the vicarage, as that discussion had been confidential.

"Are you sure you won't stay for some lunch," Caldwell asked, taking Daisy's hand in his.

"Thank you Gera... Marcus, but I'm already running late," *and besides,* Daisy thought, *I need to consider whether I can trust you in the light of everything you've told me.*

"Of course, well, I hope you sleep better, and that we can speak again very soon," the man seemed desperate now for some reassurance that he hadn't burnt his bridges with regard to their personal relationship, but Daisy simply smiled and nodded as he saw her out the main door onto Cobble Wynd.

If her feelings towards the florist had been too complicated to even admit to herself before his own admission, they were a jumbled mess now. Daisy

shoved them back in their metaphorical box labelled
'confusing emotions' and hurried away, oblivious to
the pining eyes of the man who watched her go.

12. POSH SANDWICHES AND SHORTBREAD

Daisy was in a world of her own as she hurried down Cobble Wynd. Between random thoughts such as *how is Bunch so good with flowers?* And *it's best to keep calling him Bunch even to myself so I don't slip up in public,* to *the only bit of the florist's that still looks the same is ironically the display of glass vases in the main shop where I found Gran bashed over the head with one,* Daisy was paying no attention to where she was going. In a moment that felt eerily like déjà-vu, the vicar felt rather than saw herself collide with someone else, though fortunately this time she didn't end up splayed out on the cobbles.

"Watch out!" The brusque warning came from a man

Daisy instantly recognised as Bea's dad, older and greyer, but definitely him. He was older than her mum by at least a decade. The angry scowl was Daniel Harper's go-to expression with Daisy. Even during childhood, Daisy didn't need to crash into the man to provoke it. It had been years since they had seen each other in person – over a decade in fact – yet he obviously hadn't got over his innate dislike of her.

"Sorry, I never seem to learn," Daisy fumbled her way through the apology, thinking retrospectively that he would probably have no idea she was referring to her accident the previous week. As usual, the man simply glared at her and stormed off, as if Daisy wasn't worth his attention. It had bothered her at first, during their primary school days when she would go to Bea's house for tea and would wonder what she had done to displease the adult. The family had lived in Lillymouth then, before moving to Whitby when Harper got his promotion in the police force. Given that Lillymouth was too small a town to have its own high school, Daisy and Bea had still ended up together in the next stage of their education, and had remained fast friends despite the man's dislike of his daughter's choice. Morag had always been kind and motherly, and when Daisy reached her teens she had wondered whether some of that wasn't simply to compensate for her husband's unfounded rudeness.

Pushing the unfortunate collision out of her mind, where she simply didn't have the space for one more dissatisfied person, Daisy resumed her own inner monologue. *Could she trust a man like Bunch who could lie to everyone for over fifteen years and who is obsessive about personal gain? Is it the wealth or just the thrill of the discovery he craves? Or the fame it would garner him in treasure seeking circles? Wasn't she herself just as bad obsessing over Gran's murder...* and on and on.

It was nearly four o'clock when Daisy realised her stomach was rumbling from the lack of any food over the course of the day. She had visited old Mrs. Harrington in her townhouse on The Parade, where every Monday Daisy was offered a biscuit from the same 1970s tin that was never emptied nor refilled. As usual, she had taken pity on her digestive system and politely declined. Then it was onto Herbert Jennings on Herriot Row, who never offered the vicar so much as a glass of water for her trouble, yet proceeded to elaborate on a detailed list of the week's complaints for over an hour each time. So, the sight of the new deli that had opened in the autumn near the bottom of Cobble Wynd was a welcome interval on Daisy's way to visit Joe next down by the seafront. She popped in and bought two posh sandwiches and a couple of pieces of millionaire's shortbread for them both.

The tide was in and the white waves pummelled the beach close to the small building where her 'uncle' had his coffee shop and home. Daisy took a moment to breathe in the fresh air and to let the crashing sounds of nature ground her.

"You'll freeze if you stand there any longer," the familiar voice came to her from the cottage door.

"I'm hoping some fresh sea air will knock some sense into me," Daisy quipped back, "perhaps you should try it!"

"I see you've heard about my run-in with the pillock from the train station," Joe said as Daisy followed him into his tiny sitting room, "not that there's much to say on the matter. He just needed a few things pointing out to him, that's all."

"Like?" Daisy affected her sternest tone.

"That if he ever touches my Daisy again he won't live long enough to regret it," Joe said nonchalantly as he pushed the plunger down on a cafetière of coffee.

"Joe!" Daisy exclaimed, "You can't go about

threatening people."

"I can if they hurt someone I love. Now, tell me about your day," he effectively drew a line under the subject Daisy had come to discuss, preventing her from chastising the man further.

It felt good to be loved and looked out for, though, so Daisy let the matter drop. There had been no harm done, after all. Joe had been spending the winter months, when The Boathouse coffee shop was closed for half the week, indulging in his main passion of painting, and Daisy admired his recent canvases. It was lovely to sit with her feet up and talk about things other than parish affairs for a while. In particular, Daisy pushed from her thoughts her next appointment – the last of the day – which was beginning to loom large whenever there was a lull in conversation.

"You seem distracted, Daisy," Joe said, putting down the painting he had been showing her.

"I'm fine," Daisy gave her pat response.

"You forget I've known you since you were a tiny thing, Daisy Bloom. Spill, what's on your mind?"

Daisy would never divulge private information, such as the apparently blossoming relationship between

Tallie and Anthony Glendinning, or the young woman's reason for accepting his advances, so she tried to skirt the real issues by saying, "I've to meet Anthony Glendinning at the Crow's Nest Inn, and to be honest, it's not a conversation I want to have."

"About how he invited those travellers up here in the first place? Because he should take some responsibility you know, for persuading them to move on and..."

"Yes, something like that," Daisy interrupted, already getting indigestion from the light meal they'd just shared.

"Well, you give it to him both barrels, Daisy, we don't need their likes round here. In fact, how about I join you both, I could..."

"No! No thank you. I, ah, can't be being seen as not able to perform my parish duties. It would get back to Robert Briggs and he would..."

"You're not having more trouble with him are you? I've told you, a restraining order would be the best way..."

"No, no, all blown over," they seemed to just keep interrupting each other, and Daisy was fast becoming weary with the conversation. It was lovely to have a father figure – until it wasn't!

The vicar left twenty minutes earlier than she'd
planned in the hopes of clearing her head on the way
to the pub, keen to draw a line under the whole day.
The setting winter sun had turned the sky shades of
orange and red, and Daisy sent a heartfelt prayer
heavenward that Anthony would have had second
thoughts about his intentions to marry Tallie. It wasn't
her place to share the young woman's own
circumstances, though she was pretty sure Anthony
had worked them out. *Perhaps he has a knight in shining
armour complex?* Daisy wondered, *Wanting to ride in on
his proverbial white horse and save the poor maiden.*
Whatever his motivations, Daisy planned to try to
dissuade the man from the matrimonial course of
action he'd proposed. How she would do that, though,
she really had no idea.

13. GRATEFUL FOR SMALL MERCIES

Anthony was already waiting at a table in the corner when Daisy entered the Crow's Nest Inn, a nearly drunk pint of what looked like coke in front of him, and an empty half pint glass as if he'd recently had some company. Daisy gave him a quick wave and then ordered a small lemonade and lime from Gemma at the bar, having seen her dad, Billy, leaving as she entered.

"Can I get you another?" Daisy asked as she took her seat opposite the man.

"No thanks, reverend, I drove here, better stay off the strong stuff. I might get another coke in a mo. Thanks for meeting me. I'm assuming it all went well with Tallie yesterday? You managed to get everything in your diary?"

Daisy took a large gulp of her soft drink and felt the bubbles explode up her nose, "Well, it's not exactly that simple, I'm afraid."

"Oh?" The man's forehead furrowed and he leaned forwards, half across the table, the easy air he'd been affecting since her arrival disappeared, "And why would that be?"

"Well, let's see," Daisy tried to summon her most professional demeanour and willed herself not to feel belittled by her companion's steely glare, "There is the issue that Tallie is in a relationship with another man and is carrying his child…"

Before she could say more, Anthony jumped in, "Did she say that was an issue? That she wanted to stay with him?" His raised voice garnered them some looks from the folk on nearby tables, and Daisy could only imagine how this encounter would set the gossip machine grinding.

"Well, I am bound to keep the exact contents of our discussion private, so you would have to ask her," this was not going at all as the vicar had intended.

"Look vicar, ah Daisy," the man had an altogether

more obsequious tone now. He steepled his hands on the table between them and tilted his head for maximum effect, "I know I may come across as flighty or whatever, but I can assure you my travelling days are over. I want to settle down – with Tallie, of course – and soon I'll have the means to do that."

Daisy didn't ask about his implied financial upturn, that not being a prerequisite for marriage after all and so really none of her business. But she'd be lying if she said her curiosity wasn't piqued. Aloud, she replied, "Your future plans are more Tallie's concern than mine, Mr. Glendinning, I just have to perform my professional duty in a way that my own conscience will allow."

Although the statement was deliberately vague, the meaning was not lost on Glendinning. He pursed his lips in displeasure, in an expression rather too reminiscent of his mother, and stood abruptly.

"Well, vicar, there are plenty of other churches in nearby towns and the town hall even as a last resort. Thank you for your time."

Daisy gave the man a moment to leave, watching as the pub door crashed shut behind him, and then picked up her bag a mere minute later. Her almost untouched drink now forgotten as the pain in her body reared its ugly head telling the vicar she'd been out of the house for far too long and needed to head for home whilst she still had the energy to do so under her own steam.

Daisy walked the short distance down Crow's Nest Lane and turned onto the ancient stone bridge known as St. Mary's Chare. Ahead of her, she could see Anthony Glendinning, his woollen hat pulled low over his head, his heavy, fast gait betraying his anger. A way beyond him, coming towards them from the other side of the bridge was another tall, broad figure. Daisy didn't have time to study that person any further, even as they were illuminated by the light of the old lamp that stood proudly at the end of the narrow road, as a car came screeching down from the direction of the town square, aiming directly for the bridge but driving recklessly, as if the driver didn't quite have the vehicle under control.

The car swung to the side, which Daisy assumed in the moment was an attempt to avoid the figure of the man ahead of Anthony, until that is it took a violent adjustment in order to be driving straight at him. In that brief second, when the vicar was filled with horror and couldn't even shout a warning past her own shock, the man was mowed down.

The grinding noise of a gearbox trying to find reverse filled the air, and for that moment the vehicle was stationary, giving Daisy a chance to study it. Shielding her eyes against the harsh glare from its headlamps, and rushing forward, ignoring her cane which had clattered to the ground, Daisy was sure it was Violet Glendinning's Audi that she saw. The son of the woman in question had rushed ahead to attend to the man who was lying on the ground and was paying no attention to the car, whilst Daisy was hurrying to join him as fast as she could without her walking aid. Looking up, as the car managed to turn ready to head back the way it had come, Daisy registered the familiar private number plate VI0 L3T and the bright red hat on the driver's head, before the car disappeared with a screeching of tires and engine smoke.

"I really don't have any more details than that," Daisy stumbled over the words in her tiredness. She had been sitting in the back of Detective Cluero's car for the past half an hour, answering questions from both him and the uniformed female officer who also sat up front. Thankfully, Detective Michelle Matlock had chosen to take Anthony Glendinning down to the police station for a statement, meaning Daisy didn't have to deal with her high school nemesis. *I suppose I should be grateful for small mercies,* she told herself.

The injured man, who had turned out to be Jugger, was sadly pronounced dead at the scene and had been taken away an hour ago, for autopsy Daisy presumed. She thought it strange that a hit and run should cause outright death, as normally the injured person at least managed to get to hospital for treatment, even if they passed away later. That had been the case for her own mum, Daisy knew, although she had been very young at the time. Years later, when she had understood enough to question her gran, she had been given the basic details of the tragic incident.

Her mum's killer had never been found, but Daisy didn't think that would be the case here. She had felt not a small amount of guilt telling Cluero that she was eighty percent certain it was Violet Glendinning's car that she had seen, as if she were condemning the woman – not a place any member of the cloth wanted to find themselves in. She knew she should try to remain impartial in criminal enquiries, but Daisy had to be honest. So, she had described exactly what she saw, even as the detective's eyebrows were nearly in his hairline in surprise by the time the vicar had finished.

"We'll need to speak to you some more, in the

morning, and take a formal statement," the Welshman said, unable to suppress his own yawn, "in the meantime, let's drive you home, Vicar."

"Thank you," Daisy whispered, only now realising that her walking stick still lay on the ground on the bridge where it had fallen. She was desperate to get back to the vicarage, even though it meant facing Sylvia's own inquisition, and couldn't face asking if she could get her cane if it meant she wouldn't get a lift home. So, Daisy said nothing, knowing she'd have to use her hospital-issued spare the next day.

It had been the longest of Mondays, and Daisy had a feeling the week was about to get worse before it got better.

14. YOU CAN CALL ME ANYTHING YOU LIKE

"And it was a red hat, you say," Sylvia asked over breakfast the next morning. She was typing on her phone at the time, only looking up intermittently to encourage Daisy to keep talking, and the vicar had the distinct impression that her housekeeper was sharing their conversation in her chat group with the book club ladies. When she asked her if that was actually the case, Sylvia affected an air of complete innocence and, with all the indignant confidence of someone who wants you to believe they've been falsely accused, tucked the device into her apron.

Daisy was lacking in patience. And sleep, for that

matter, having had her worst night since Christmas. She had tossed and turned for hours, ignoring text messages from Joe and Gerald that had pinged onto her phone first thing this morning, no doubt as soon as the two men heard about the events of last night. Daisy knew she couldn't put them off for long, however, if she didn't want them simply turning up on the vicarage doorstep.

As if conjured by her thoughts, the doorbell went at that very moment, causing a round of church bells from Archie and a slow stretch from Jacob, who had been dosing on Daisy's lap. Unannounced visitors were not worthy of the cat's quicker reactions, which were generally reserved for food-related excitement.

"Who would be here so early?" The housekeeper tutted as she went to open the door, still in her hair curlers and satin headscarf. Checking her own phone, however, Daisy saw it was actually half past nine and most people would have already started their working day.

Sending up a quick prayer request that it wasn't either of the local detectives, Daisy was only slightly relieved when she heard Morag Harper's voice.

"Daisy did say to pop round this morning," the vicar heard the woman explain to Sylvia, prompting her own memory that she had made the arrangement back at church on Sunday.

"Yes, come in," Daisy called through, heaving herself off the kitchen chair to the protestation of her back and hips. She sucked in a breath, trying to control her reaction to the intense shooting pain, and adjusted her expression so that hopefully none of that would show as she greeted their guest.

When the required pot of tea and plate of biscuits had been served, and Sylvia had excused herself to finish getting dressed, Daisy began with an apology, "I'm so sorry I forgot about your visit, Morag, it was an eventful evening yesterday."

It seemed that Bea's mum was the only one in the town to not have heard of the death of one of the activists, and so Daisy gave her a brief recap.

"My goodness, Daisy, you must be shattered! I can go and come back another day..."

"No, no, I'm happy to see you. I'm guessing you're staying over at the Book Nook with Bea?"

"Yes, just till she's properly back on her feet. I did persuade her to speak to the health visitor last week, in case there's maybe some postnatal depression mixed up with everything that's going on. And of course, I love the time with Daisy Mae…"

At the mention of the little girl who was no longer – had never actually officially been – her goddaughter, Daisy couldn't help the tears which filled her eyes. Tiredness made her more emotional anyway, but the vicar couldn't hide her hurt.

"Oh Daisy, I'm so sorry. I did try to counsel against it at the time, but Bea insisted her cousin should be godmother and Daisy Mae should be christened as quickly as possible."

"It's not your fault, Morag, really, I'm just sad it came to this, that's all."

"I know, you were always such firm friends and I'm sure you can be again, just give her time."

"I will, I will," Daisy paused to blow her nose, "anyway, I wanted to tell you about an idea I had for the bookshop – well, more of an outreach project actually. It relies on the steam engine rides going ahead in a few months."

"Well, I'm sure you'll have no more trouble from those activists now their leader has gone," Morag said bluntly, "I'd assume the others will soon disappear."

Daisy thought of Tallie and felt a pang of worry, though she didn't mention the young woman, "Yes, we can hope so, and so my idea was that before the attraction even opens, Andrew could put himself forward at the council meeting to do the repairs on the waiting room and station buildings – they'll need a good joiner, as most of the fascias and mouldings in the old place are wood – and then when it opens, Bea could get the licence to sell refreshments from the kiosk, along with guide books of the local area, postcards and such like. Maybe a loyalty scheme whereby if you buy one there, you get a free hot drink in the Book Nook or something. That would bring them some income as well as publicising the shop so that hopefully the visitors will stop in there too."

"Wow, Daisy, that is a fantastic idea! Thank you, but you must tell Bea yourself."

"No, no, she won't want to hear my suggestions at the moment. Just pass it off as your own. Please Morag.

"Aye lass, well, I'm not happy with it, but okay. Just till you two have reconciled, mind, then I'll tell her the truth."

They were interrupted then by the doorbell and Morag stood to leave, "I won't take up any more of your time, Daisy, thank you for being such a good friend to Bea."

She hugged the vicar which had the tears flowing again and opened the door to find Bunch on the doorstep.

Following behind, Daisy said her goodbyes and then invited the florist in, knowing by the dark look on the man's face that she should have at least texted back to reassure him she was okay. Bunch didn't visit the vicarage often – in fact Daisy could count the number of times he had on one hand – partly due to his animal allergies but mainly because of her housekeeper's rather military gatekeeping skills. Very few who were not invited actually made it across the threshold of the old cottage.

"Daisy, you've been crying," the statement, though spoken gently, was still accusatory in nature and had the vicar immediately going on the defensive.

"Yes well, Morag and I were discussing little Daisy Mae and... Anyway, what can I do for you, Gerald or Marcus or... look I'm just going to stick to Gerald Bunch okay, so I don't trip myself up with anyone."

"You can call me anything you like, Daisy, if it will stop you taking that officious tone with me. We're closer than that, aren't we? I'm just worried about you, the bags under your eyes alone are twice as dark and deep as they were yesterday, telling me you've had another sleepless night. Please let me do what I can to support you," he held out a conciliatory hand and Daisy took it, allowing herself to be pulled into the hug which followed. Annoyed that she could hear herself sniffling once again and that the man's chest felt altogether too warm and safe, she quickly pulled back.

"Okay, Gerald, let's have some coffee shall we? And refrain from any more comments on my ghastly appearance. No doubt you've come to hear about last night."

"Only in the respect of whether you're doing okay, I couldn't care less about that feeble excuse for a man who got run over."

Daisy raised her eyebrow at the man's lack of Christian caring, but said nothing as she filled the kettle, imagining most of the locals would have the same opinion, harsh as it may be.

No sooner had the pair sat down at the table with their drinks than the doorbell went again. Sylvia was still upstairs in her room beautifying herself and the mynah bird chose that moment to let everyone know he was annoyed at his morning nap being disturbed.

"Here, you stay there, I'll get it," Gerald said, to the grating noise of a make believe police chase coming from the boot room, complete with profanities, sirens and gun shots.

"No more cop dramas for you!" Daisy shouted through to the noisy bird, just as another kerfuffle broke out on the doorstep.

"What the heck are you doing here? I've told you before not to bother her, you creepy letch," Uncle Joe's voice drifted through to the kitchen when Archie finally ceased his racket.

"Oh no!" Daisy shot up from her seat, aggravating the joints that were already partially seized up from yesterday, "It's okay, Joe, he just came to check on me!"

Of course, no one knew – or could know – of the growing friendship between the vicar and florist, which Daisy knew was going to make explaining this difficult.

"Simply a concerned parishioner," Bunch said in his loud, boorish tone, "we can't have this lovely lady wanting to leave town, can we?"

"Surely you can't want him here, lass?" Joe pushed

past Gerald and stood in front of Daisy beside the antique coat stand.

Faced with both men and their equally expectant expressions, Daisy sighed heavily.

"I was just about to leave," Bunch said, breaking the tension of the awkward standoff. Daisy could've kissed the man then, and the thought made her blush hotly.

"You don't have to," she whispered, as Joe stomped into the kitchen, considering himself having won.

"We can't talk when anyone else is around anyway. I knew I was taking a risk coming here," Gerald stroked some flyaway bits of hair off Daisy's face. She could only imagine what she looked like, having not even redone her plait from yesterday, let alone brushed her hair or washed her face, "I just needed to see with my own eyes that you're okay."

"I'll stop by the shop later," Daisy promised, "probably after dinner this evening."

"Only if you're up to it, love," he kissed her tenderly on the forehead and then left, leaving Daisy holding onto the doorframe and feeling slightly bereft.

"Since when do you decide who can and can't come into my home, Joe?" Daisy demanded the moment she was back in the kitchen, "Besides, this is a vicarage, it's open to the public!"

"Aye well, not on my watch, and not when there's been more violence in the town," Joe stood his ground, increasing the vicar's exasperation.

When the doorbell went again at that very moment, Daisy felt like she might explode. She heard Sylvia shouting "I'm coming" from the top of the stairs, followed by a shriek as the housekeeper apparently tripped over her own house rabbit. This set Jacob off, who barely tolerated the white wanderer at the best of times, and he charged up the stairs yowling, whilst the mynah bird started shrieking "Happy Birthday" for goodness only knew what reason.

Daisy slumped back into her usual chair with her head in her hands, and Joe hurried to check Sylvia was okay.

"Sounded like you're busy so I let myself in."

Of course, it would be Michelle Matlock who would arrive during the chaos, a wry, smug smile on her face as she stood in the doorway viewing the defeated slump of Daisy's body against the kitchen table.

15. BANG TO RIGHTS!

"Detective Matlock, what a pleasure," Daisy couldn't keep the sarcasm from her voice as she stood slowly under the pretence of refilling the kettle. Anything to keep her hands occupied and her back to the woman whose presence she could barely tolerate even at the best of times. Oh, Daisy was well aware it wasn't Christian of her. That she should forgive and forget, turn the other cheek and all that. But where Michelle Matlock was concerned, Daisy's well of forgiveness ran dry a long time ago.

"I can do that, Vicar," Sylvia said rather chidingly, floating into the kitchen with her hair immaculately coiffed and her red lipstick perfectly applied.

Daisy bit her tongue, turning to see Joe giving the detective the full force of his fatherly glare. He knew what the teenage version of the woman in front of him had done to torment Daisy in her formative years, and had clearly not forgotten either.

"You've got a friend in me," Archie piped up, flying through from the boot room to land on Joe's shoulder.

"Get out of it," the man scolded, jiggling his arm to encourage the bird to move on, "it's like a blummin' zoo in here."

"Isn't it just," Michelle agreed with a wry smile, giving Daisy the distinct impression she wasn't just talking about the animals.

Once Joe had been dispatched home with as much tact and reassurance as Daisy could manage, and Sylvia had retreated to the sitting room after Daisy had assured her that of course the situation didn't warrant her missing her morning fix of 'Police, Camera, Action,' the vicar resumed her position at the kitchen table. Detective Matlock sat opposite, a pot of Yorkshire's finest and two slices of lemon drizzle cake between them as if to enforce the civility of the encounter. For they were nothing if not British!

Daisy had no patience for the icy silence, the stretching

tension, and quickly initiated the discussion, if only to get it over with and the odious woman out of her home, "So, Detective, I presume you're here to ask me about last night's tragic accident."

"Quite so, Vicar, though I think we can immediately dispense with referring to it as an accident. I think we both know it was an intentional assault, and that the perpetrator was Her Haughtiness Mrs. Glendinning."

Of course, the detective was familiar with Violet, having grown up in the town and been subject to the woman's wrath on more than one occasion. Daisy had a feeling Mrs. Glendinning was not a stranger to the police in recent times either, aways having a grievance to report on one of her neighbours and suchlike.

"Well, ah, as I told your colleague last night, I merely saw the car, and even then I can't be one hundred percent sure. Have you traced the vehicle?"

"We found it dumped down the back of Pease's Lane. Dent in the front bumper and all."

"And it belongs to Violet Glendinning?"

"It does. Can you remember what hat the lady in question wore to your church service on Sunday morning."

"Ah, well," Daisy tried to play for time, though she knew that no delay would be long enough to conceal the truth. The police had clearly been given a witness statement detailing the accessory anyway, "that's a rather random question, but yes, it was quite striking. Knitted in Red... with, ah, feathers of the same colour."

"As we thought, thank you, Vicar, do let me know if you happen to see the accessory in the course of your parish visits," Matlock was all professional now, none of the personal jibes of earlier.

Like a bloodhound who has scented its quarry, Daisy thought, but kept it to herself.

"But why would Violet... I mean, what could have come over her? She'd had her altercations with the man, to be sure, but..."

"Oh? Tell me more about those."

Daisy gulped, she had well and truly dropped Violet in it now. She proceeded to detail Violet's views on the newcomers, as voiced in the parish council meetings which were all minuted anyway, hoping she could avoid explaining the incident where she herself had been knocked down in the street and Violet had been witness to the ensuing fisticuffs. Her reticence was in vain, however, as seemingly the detective already knew about the whole event, her smug smile now returning as she asked if Daisy was fully recovered.

"Yes, I'm quite well, thank you," Daisy replied tersely.

"Very good. We will of course need a signed statement down at the station. Oh, and one last thing, Vicar, did Mrs. Glendinning ever mention visiting the activists in the waiting room where they had set up camp?"

Daisy racked her brain, "Not directly, she ah, did say that it smelt like a pigsty as I recall, so I assumed she had paid them a visit."

Matlock smiled like the proverbial cat that got the cream, and Daisy knew instantly that she had said the wrong thing – well, for Violet anyway.

"Thank you, Vicar, I'll show myself out."

"But, ah, I can't be sure she went there, I mean…" Daisy began rambling and stuttering, but the policewoman was already at the door.

"Bang to rights!" Archie gave his view as the front door slammed shut and Daisy dropped her head into her hands.

"I just don't understand what would possess the

woman to do something so... so blatant," Daisy said to Sylvia over a late lunch in the kitchen, "I mean, she may not be likeable, but she's intelligent."

"Aye well, when you've seen as many crime shows as me, you soon realise – there's nowt as strange as folk," Sylvia said, nodding sagely as if to impart some extra wisdom to her words, "And Maggie Buckley, down at the tourist info office has a theory that..."

Daisy had to admit to tuning out. She sipped her fifth cup of tea of the day and wondered when the interminable drizzle outside the window would stop. The hit and run collision had brought up some long-buried feelings about her own mother's death at the tender age of twenty and whether that had truly been an accident. She had asked Gran when she'd reached that difficult pre-teen stage and felt herself mature enough to handle anything the world threw at her, and received the same three basic facts that Daisy would come to hear over the next few years. Hit while leaving work at a restaurant in Whitby. No witnesses. Police said it was very unlikely to have been pre-meditated. At first, Daisy hadn't wanted to admit that she didn't understand what that meant – pre-meditated – but as she grew older and her comprehension increased, she had become fixated for a while on whether the driver had even slowed down, maybe got out of the car to check on her mum, whether they had followed her story in the paper and found out she had died from her injuries. Surely they must've been rushing to some life and death situation that prevented them from phoning for help... Unfortunately, during her work as a victim support officer, Daisy had later come to learn that some people simply have no compassion, no inherent sense of right and wrong, feel no guilt. And, scarily, they are often the people who on first acquaintance come across as the most pleasant.

The sound of the doorbell drew her back to the room, and a short, sharp pang of dread filled the vicar. She had come to associate that particular noise with unwelcome visitors – a bit unfortunate when you live in a vicarage. Sylvia reluctantly paused her interminable monologue, tut-tutted, and rose to open the front door.

"Oh, for a moment's peace," the housekeeper muttered to herself.

Oh indeed, Daisy thought sardonically.

16. A STRANGE CONUNDRUM

Daisy had planned to spend the afternoon in her church office writing her weekly sermon, catching up on admin and correspondence and lighting a prayer candle in the main chapel for Jugger. She had barely known the man, and had wanted to further their acquaintance even less, but still he was a human being who had now gone to meet his Maker, and Daisy intended to say a prayer for the man's soul. It was God's place to judge him, not hers, Daisy reminded herself when she found herself appalled at the thought she might have to conduct a funeral service for the awful man.

Distracted by these thoughts as she lit the match, Daisy

didn't hear the footsteps of someone approaching through the vestry until they had almost reached her.

"Violet! You gave me a fright!" The vicar exclaimed as she felt the light touch on her shoulder, the hairs on her neck standing on end as she spun around to see the familiar figure, the small flame going out as she did so.

"My apologies, Vicar, I thought you had heard me. The front doors were locked, so I came in the back way."

Daisy studied Violet's hunched frame, the dark circles under her eyes, and the mis-matched shoes and handbag – normally a crime in that woman's book – and felt a small amount of pity.

"I thought you would be at the police station still," Daisy spoke bluntly.

"I've not long been released. They're checking the CCTV, taking statements and suchlike. I'm not allowed to leave Lillymouth," on the last word, the woman's high-pitched voice wobbled and Daisy could tell she was struggling to hold on to her composure. "They said I was only free to go at all because of my previous unblemished record and social standing."

"Well, it's all very sad," Daisy said, using one of her 'stock phrases' that she had been practising since deciding to join the clergy, and which didn't say much about anything, certainly not her personal opinion on any subject.

Violet nodded, then whipped out a brightly coloured object from behind her back, causing Daisy to stumble backwards, "I think this may be yours?" The woman said, brandishing the vicar's stick like a sword.

"Oh! Yes, but how did you..?"

"I wanted to see where it had taken place, this, this, crime they're accusing me of," Violet replied.

Daisy really didn't think that was a good idea – it could easily be misconstrued by the police as trying to tamper with evidence or something – but she didn't voice this thought, simply taking the stick and laying it on the nearest pew, "Thank you."

"You're welcome, Vicar," Violet paused and hovered on the spot uncomfortably, giving Daisy the distinct impression she hadn't just come to return the walking aid, "I, ah, I assume that since your stick was on the bridge that you were witness to the, ah, crash?"

Daisy wasn't sure what the right answer would be but, seeing as the evidence spoke for itself, she responded in the affirmative with a brisk nod.

"I see," Violet continued, "you know, they told me Anthony has made a statement saying it was me he saw."

"Really?" Daisy couldn't believe the man would drop his own mother in it like that, but he had been closer to Jugger than she was, and therefore closer to the street lamp. Perhaps he had seen the driver's face. But to give a conclusive statement to that effect, well...

"That's what the detective told me," Violet sank onto the pew, but Daisy chose to remain standing despite her hip protesting the long time on her feet.

"Perhaps they were just trying to get a confession?" The vicar suggested gently, "You didn't give them one did you?"

"Of course not!" Violet snapped, "I'm not going to confess to something I didn't do!"

And you're not going to get much sympathy talking to people like that, Daisy thought. Aloud she said, "Well, what did you tell them?"

"That I was at home by myself all evening as Percy was out with his golf buddies, that I didn't realise my car had moved, as far as I knew it was on the street outside. Then I answered all their questions –

interminable questions wanting to know whether I'd been to the train station recently..."

"And had you?" Daisy asked.

"No! Not once. Why would I want to visit that rabble?"

Daisy knew this to be a lie, given Violet's comment about the smell of the place when they were at the parish council meeting. If the woman could be less than honest about this, then Daisy wasn't sure she could trust her version of events at all.

Catching herself before she said more, Violet looked up at Daisy, yesterday's make-up now smudged around the woman's eyes and collected in her wrinkles giving her a neglected clown-like appearance, "Look Vicar, ah, Daisy, I came to ask if you would help me? Help me to clear my name? You know I'm not capable of mowing someone down in cold blood. Even if it was my car, it categorically wasn't me driving the blasted thing! You know on The Parade we don't have driveways, and I'd never leave it in the back alley, so anyone could have taken it..."

"Without keys?" Daisy interrupted, "And we don't exactly have a high rate of car crime in the area, Violet," the vicar was playing Devil's advocate, nevertheless it had the required effect and the woman's face fell.

"I'm going to have hell's own job proving my innocence, aren't I?" Violet sniffed.

"Maybe the CCTV will show something?" Daisy tried to sound hopeful, though the very short route between the Glendinning's home and St. Mary's Chare where the incident took place was unlikely to have many cameras – this wasn't a big city and there were no shops on that bit of road who might have their own security devices. "Or you could ask Anthony to be more specific about what he told them and what exactly he saw."

"They've told me I'm not allowed to talk to him! My own son! That he's to stay in a B&B until the matter is settled one way or another."

Daisy didn't know what to think. She wondered if the idea of Violet as the driver wasn't just too obvious, too clear-cut, but then what was the alternative? One of the local men who had a problem with Jugger – Billy? Joe? Bunch? And did she really want to get more involved than she already was?

"Look Violet, I will see what I can find out in the natural course of my visits and church duties, but beyond that I'm obliged to remain impartial," Daisy hedged.

"Thank you, Vicar," the stiff upper lip was back along with Violet's terse, formal tone, and Daisy considered herself dismissed, even though she was standing in her own place of work and it was Violet who was stalking off the way she had come.

What a strange conundrum, Daisy thought as she finally lit the candle and tried to pray positively for the man she knew to have been an angry and abusive individual. Adding on a quick prayer for her own guidance and peace of mind, Daisy returned to her office feeling even more disquieted in spirit than she had earlier.

And what of the others? She wondered, making a mental note to visit Tallie the next day, assuming the young woman was still staying at the train station. With her, at least, the vicar hoped to make a positive difference.

17. GOLDILOCKS

Daisy balanced her umbrella in one hand and her walking stick in the other as she made her way along Church Street and onto Cobble Wynd. Ordinarily, she didn't bother with shielding her head from the incessant heavy drizzle that was common at this time of year, but having just washed and blow-dried her hair, and left her blonde locks free of a braid for the first time in memory, she wasn't having all her hard work ruined now! Daisy didn't let herself ponder why she wanted to make a special effort with her appearance, though the double-take that Sylvia had done when she saw the vicar was enough to let her know that the difference was striking enough to be noted.

Eager not to be spotted going into the side door to the florist's – the one that led straight to the flat above – and setting idle tongues a-wagging, Daisy had sent a text message to Bunch notifying him of her imminent arrival. So she found the door slightly ajar when she got there and let herself in.

"Gerald, it's just me," Daisy called out as she heaved herself up the steep, narrow staircase. A fleeting memory, of herself as a young girl flying up these steps, assailed Daisy and for a brief second she could almost feel the lightness of body and spirit which the innocent Daisy of her childhood had enjoyed. It brought a sudden lump to her throat, and the vicar chided herself silently for her foolish emotions.

"Come straight up, love," Gerald's voice returned her greeting, and before Daisy had reached the top landing the man himself was there to greet her.

Giving Daisy a moment to catch her breath, the florist opened his arms tentatively, and she walked straight into them as if like a moth to a flame. Not wanting to dwell on her traitorous legs, which had overridden any sensible thought to put some distance between them, Daisy allowed herself a few brief seconds of peace and tranquillity in the man's embrace. Gone were the anxious thoughts, the panicked fluttering in her chest which were an ever-present companion, as Daisy allowed herself to just be.

"What's this?" Bunch whispered, lowering his face to Daisy's head. If she weren't mistaken, the vicar had the sensation that the man was smelling her newly-washed locks. Certainly, she was sure he was running a gentle hand down her silky tresses. Instead of pulling away, as Daisy would have assumed would be her reaction to such an intimate gesture, she instead found herself rooted to the spot, arms around the man's waist, a small ball of happiness and warmth growing in her chest that he had noticed her efforts. The seconds drew out into a minute and neither seemed keen to move.

"Oh, it was due a wash," Daisy whispered in reply, tilting her head up so that her words wouldn't be muffled in the man's waistcoat, and feeling the heat in her chest rise to her cheeks.

"It's beautiful, you're beautiful Daisy," Bunch replied, his face hovering above hers as if he might just...

Whether it was the rare flattery, which Daisy's own self-image wouldn't let her believe to be true, or the near proximity which hinted at further intimacies to come, Daisy couldn't be sure – either way, the result was the same as the vicar stepped quickly and firmly out of the man's grasp and to the side, making a show of taking off her coat. If Bunch was disappointed he didn't let on, dropping his arms quickly and simply following Daisy's lead of acting as if the 'moment' – whatever it was – had not happened.

The vicar refused the offer of a glass of wine. Not because she was tee-total, which she certainly was not, but rather because the last thing she needed right now was something that would further lower her inhibitions. Instead she opted for a cup of Yorkshire tea and a ginger snap – much safer, she hoped. Bunch also took the sensible option and sat on the armchair across from the sofa on which Daisy was perched. Happy with his choice, the vicar allowed herself to relax into the couch and balanced her mug on her knee.

"So, that self-righteous old bag has finally got her comeuppance?" Gerald phrased it as a question, but the venom in his tone was unmissable leading Daisy to wonder what run-ins the man had had with Violet in the past.

"Well, it seems that way, but something just doesn't seem right to me. I mean, why would she do something so obvious? Not even trying to hide her guilt? So public, and in her own car of all things? Violet may be haughty and judgemental, but she's not stupid."

"Aye well, at least that oaf's death will have put paid to their treasure hunting," there was no compassion in the man's voice, and Daisy wondered again at the extent of Bunch's obsession with the supposed hoards buried beneath the town.

Choosing to change the subject rather than address his uncharitable comment, Daisy took the opportunity to ask a question which had long been burning in the back of her mind – since the night the florist had saved her from Rob Briggs, in fact.

"So, ah, speaking of treasure hunting, you never did tell me what you were doing in the graveyard with a shovel that night you ah, saved me."

"What? Oh," Bunch paused, as if assessing how much to divulge before releasing a small sigh and opting for full disclosure, "well, the old maps show the tunnels as continuing beyond this shop, under Cobble Wynd and actually all the way to the churchyard. I suppose that would've been a quiet place where people expected night-time digging in the past so it would've been easier to begin them there. I was hoping to find some evidence of the opening and…"

"Gerald, you can't go digging on consecrated ground!" Daisy replied, horrified.

"I didn't disturb any of the plots, I…"

"Still!" The vicar interrupted again.

They both looked at each other then, in uncomfortable silence, and anxiety began to fill Daisy's chest in the same spot that just a short while ago had felt the warmth of connection and maybe even something more. She leaned forwards and set her mug on the floor beside the sofa, there being no table within reach. Then she tried to calm her breathing, the tightness in her chest receding ever so slightly with her efforts.

"Daisy, love, I'm sorry, are you okay?" Gerald moved as if to join her on the settee, but Daisy waved him off with a sharp swash of her hand.

"Tell me one thing," the vicar asked, speaking in a staccato and measured way, which was all her choppy breaths would allow, "would anything make you stop this search for treasure? Anything encourage you to give up hunting for this ultimate haul?"

Gerald reared back from his position, kneeling on the floor a few steps away from Daisy, and returned to the chair he had occupied until a few moments ago. He wiped his hair back from his forehead and adjusted his cravat. His lack of response was all the reply Daisy needed and she forced her body into a standing position to leave. Certainly, the vicar didn't expect Bunch to retort with a question of his own.

"Perhaps I will answer that when you tell me... Could you ever give up the hunt for justice for your grandmother? Will you ever rest until her killer is found?"

A small gasp escaped Daisy's mouth before she brought her hand up quickly to cover it. Her heart was racing, dizziness encroaching as she grabbed her backpack and walking stick and lurched towards the door to the top of the stairs.

"I'm sorry, Daisy, don't go, I, ah, you just touched a nerve that's all..." the man tried to backtrack, but Daisy had already begun her descent.

"I would say we're at an impasse, Gerald, no point in continuing," Daisy managed to blurt out as she rushed out into the frigid evening air, unable to stop the sob which burst from her the moment her feet touched the cobbles.

The vicar paused a moment to compose herself, expecting Bunch to join her outside and offer to walk her home, but he made no such appearance. So, with silent tears tracking down her cheeks and willing herself to return to the numbness that was her constant companion for so many years, Daisy made her way back to the vicarage, pausing only to lean against the wall of the baker's to braid her hair.

18. HIT BY A FREIGHT TRAIN

The vicar was in no mood for a foolish feline the next morning. Seeing the rotund rear of the vicarage cat deliberately bumping into her walking stick which leant against the wall in the hallway, sending it clattering to the floor, Daisy rebuked the animal sternly. All to no avail, of course, as Jacob sauntered off towards her bedroom with his tail high in the air, no doubt to give her books and papers the same treatment.

"Argh," Daisy growled as she bent to retrieve the walking aid, suffering the pain in her hip and side brought on by the effort.

"All okay, petal?" Sylvia asked from the top of the

stairs where she hovered, still not dressed.

"I'm going to the train station, to see if Tallie's still there. If not I'll try the B&B where Anthony is holed up. Either way, I'm determined to speak to her and offer her a room here for a few nights. Could you make sure the spare bed is made up?" Daisy could hear the sharp edge in her tone, and knew her housekeeper didn't deserve it, but the man who did was the last person the vicar intended to speak to this day – or any day going forward for that matter.

Sleep had eluded the vicar last night, and she had spent most of the dark hours writing in her journal. Not that it had helped to unravel her confusing feelings regarding a certain treasure seeker, however. In truth, the only purpose it had served was to solidify Daisy's conviction that she should steer well clear of matters of romantic inclination.

The waiting room at the disused train station was littered with take-away food packaging, cigarette stubs and other discarded items which the vicar didn't want to dwell on. When she arrived, it was to find Tallie kneeling on the floor, attempting to clear up the refuse.

"Tallie, I'm so happy to find you still here, though I

really think we should leave that mess up to the professionals, with you being in your current state," knowing the pregnancy was a difficult topic for the young woman, Daisy attempted to skirt around it.

"I don't mind, Badger and Aislin are long gone – one sniff of the law is all it takes to send them skittering off."

"Well, I mind, come and sit down a bit," Daisy plonked herself down on one of the original engraved wooden benches which lined the walls of the room and indicated that Tallie should join her.

With a sigh, the younger woman obliged, though she remained rigidly facing forwards whilst the vicar turned her body sideways to face her companion. Daisy let the uncomfortable silence drag out, knowing from experience that often people would eventually speak up to fill the void. In this instance, she had not been wrong and Tallie soon began talking.

"I'm not sad that he's dead," the young woman said, and Daisy could recognise the numbness in her tone, "I just wish I wasn't carrying his baby."

This wasn't the first time the former victim liaison officer had met women in this situation – the father gone from the scene for whatever reason, bringing immense relief, but a link to him still remaining with his unborn child – and she knew she had to tread carefully. As part of the clergy, Daisy now felt limited in the options she could explain and so decided to mention the refuge again, as somewhere that Tallie could receive the advice and support she needed.

"Come to the vicarage for a few days, you can't stay in this mess, and then I can take you across to Leeds."

"Anthony wants me to move in with him. He'll be coming into money soon," Tallie gasped and her hand flew to her mouth as if she had just disclosed something she wasn't meant to.

Daisy pretended this was the first time she had heard this and nodded encouragingly, "And is that what you want? To move in with him? Is his change in fortunes definite?"

"Well, ah," Tallie looked everywhere but at the vicar. Eventually her petite frame slumped back against the rigid back of the bench and she whispered, "What is it with men and treasure?"

It was a strange use of vocabulary, Daisy thought, and very specific as opposed to the more general term of 'money' and her ears pricked up.

"Treasure?" She asked as nonchalantly as possible.

"I suppose it's okay to say now Jugger's dead, but we were never really here for the environment, the steam train or whatever is planned, it was all because Jugger was part of this underground group of treasure seekers and Anthony is part of the group too, so when they met by chance and shared information... well, we ended up here. Jugger had access to some maps which Anthony thought might be the missing piece to the puzzle, though as far as I could see they were just some freezing cold caves and a random island full of seagulls and bird poo..." Now she wasn't talking about the specifics of her own predicament, the young woman's tongue seemed to have been loosened.

"Oh?" Daisy tried to keep her responses open ended.

"Yes, Anthony reckons he's better going it alone now without Jugger, that he's almost cracked it or something. I'm not sure how, since as far as I'm aware neither of them have found any evidence at all of the stories and maps being true. If you ask me..."

The conversation was cut short as the treasure hunter in question arrived then, barging through the waiting room door like a man on a mission and stopping short when he saw the vicar.

"Tallie, what have I said about talking to busybodies?" His tone was low and ominous, adding to Daisy's already churning stomach.

The talk of treasure hunting had made her think of Bunch and the lengths people might go to to eliminate any opposition to their search. Since Anthony had been within Daisy's own sights when Jugger was run over he couldn't be a suspect, but what about Bunch? Had Daisy been blinkered again as she was with the two Briggs men last year? Though this time by her own emotional attachment rather than by her suspicions about Gran's killer?

The vicar shot to her feet, her body protesting the sudden movement, as Glendinning continued speaking to Tallie as if Daisy wasn't there.

"I don't understand why you won't move into the B&B with me, love, just for a bit, this place smells like a pigsty!"

"Actually, the reverend has invited me to stay in the vicarage," the young woman's voice wobbled and her chin quivered, but she stood slowly and came to stand beside Daisy, her eyes never leaving the man's as if wary of his sudden movement.

The use of that particular description, 'pigsty,' hit

Daisy like the metaphorical freight train as she recalled Violet saying exactly the same thing at the parish council meeting and she herself using it as evidence that the woman had visited the waiting room.

What if she was simply repeating what her son had told her? What if she had never actually been in here herself and hadn't had the contact with Jugger that I assumed she had? Daisy thought silently, but she was drawn quickly back to the strained atmosphere in the room, to the man whose bushy eyebrows were bunched in anger and who advanced menacingly on the shaking girl beside her.

Putting her arm around Tallie's shoulders and squaring her own, Daisy took a step forward, sending up a silent prayer for protection for them both and then saying aloud, "Anthony, perhaps your attentions are better directed towards your mother at this time. I'm sure she could use your support. Maybe in trying to remember things from the night of the murder…"

At mention of that incident, the young woman beside her began shaking even more uncontrollably, though Daisy couldn't focus on her now. No, all her attention needed to be on the man who stood between them and the door.

"You're the parish vicar, shouldn't you be helping my

mother? And as for that night, I called out to warn the man but it all happened too fast. End of story."

"Really? I don't recall hearing you?" It came out before Daisy could measure her words. The last thing she wanted now was to anger him further.

"Well, you were a way behind me," Anthony snarled, "and who even knows what goes through my mother's head? You saw her car with your own eyes. Case closed, eh?"

Daisy had the awful feeling she was being played but had no idea how. Moving forwards, and having to practically drag Tallie with her, she replied, "Well, the police have it all in hand, I'm sure, we'd better be getting back, Sylvia will have lunch ready."

"Tallie..." Glendinning growled ominously, but Daisy ignored him, ignored the anxiety swelling in her chest and the sudden desire to run and simply side stepped the man, using her cane against his foot to put distance between them and to cause him to move out of their way.

The two women gulped in the fresh air as they hurried to Daisy's car.

"Don't look back," she whispered to Tallie, as they felt

the man's angry eyes boring into their backs, "you're safe now."

19. DIRTY LAUNDRY

Back at the vicarage, Daisy called Joe and asked if he'd mind going to the train station and retrieving Tallie's backpack, as the women had left it in their haste to leave. She had hoped to have a quiet afternoon chatting with the young woman as they settled her into the vicarage, but as usual Daisy's plans were scuppered and she was forced to leave her guest alone in the spare room. This time with the arrival of a certain Welsh detective.

"Detective Cluero, perfect timing as usual, I've just baked some fruit scones," Sylvia giggled like a schoolgirl and Daisy was half amused, half shocked at the sight of her septuagenarian housekeeper flirting with the detective who must be at least twenty years her junior.

As if it was all water off a duck's back, or he simply lacked awareness of these things, the man himself sat down heavily at the kitchen table with a sigh, "Any coffee going, Mrs. Carmichael?"

"For you, of course!" Sylvia batted her well-mascaraed eyelashes and Daisy felt the urge to laugh.

"Stronger the better would be grand," the Welshman replied, turning his attention to the vicar and doing his best to ignore the house rabbit who was staring at him scathingly from his perch atop the full washing basket in the corner.

"I'll get that lot on next, even though it's not strictly the day for the white load," Sylvia clarified, seeing Daisy's attention focused on that direction, "as I want the washing machine free to do that poor girl's clothes when Joe brings her things over later. She probably hasn't been able to wash anything properly for months."

"I doubt Tallie has much," Daisy said absentmindedly, "it could probably all be shoved in together with ours."

Sylvia tut-tutted at the idea but the vicar had already tuned her out. She hadn't been thinking about laundry in the first place, though her gaze was directed at the pet on the basket, rather her mind had been wandering to the evening of Jugger's death and to the drink she had – albeit briefly – shared with Anthony that night in the pub. Something wasn't right, but Daisy couldn't put her finger on what that might be.

"So vicar, I know we have your statement from the night of the incident, but new evidence has come to light and I was wondering if I could ask you a few more questions?"

"Of course," Daisy replied, though her voice was flat. She was resigned to these almost daily interludes into her routine at the moment.

"Well, the deceased's mobile phone shows he was sent a text message earlier that afternoon arranging a meeting in the park that evening and then another just ten minutes before the collision changing the location to the pub. Both were sent from an unknown number and were no doubt a ruse to have him walking back that way at the time the murderer planned to mow him down. Now, we initially assumed these messages must've been sent by Mrs. Glendinning as part of her premeditative preparations, having secretly found the man's number on her son's phone, but the coroner's report came back this morning and has shed new light on things."

"Oh?" Daisy's attention was renewed at that and she forced herself to tune back in fully.

"Yes, it seems the cause of death was compression to the neck. To be sure, the deceased had broken bones and internal bleeding caused by the vehicle, but according to the report these were not enough to have caused death so quickly. That is to say, without the added suffocation the man would've lived long enough to receive treatment."

"So, the person driving the car didn't kill him?" Daisy asked, shocked.

"Enough doubt has been cast on that, which is why I need to ask what you saw of Anthony Glendinning as he knelt beside the victim's body, supposedly offering help."

"Well, ah, he had his back to me and he's quite broad, so not much I'm afraid, other than he was bending forward and I couldn't see his hands."

"Think vicar, could he have had his knee on the victim's neck, or his hands around his throat?"

"I really couldn't tell you, not from the angle I was at," Daisy was getting frustrated now, "perhaps you should be questioning him?"

"Oh, you can be certain that we are. Matlock has gone to bring the man in now."

"Do you think he was in cahoots with his mother, then?" Daisy asked, incredulous, "I mean, to what end?"

"I don't have the answer to that... yet," Cluero replied, accepting the huge mug of black coffee and two warm scones from Sylvia and smiling gratefully up at her, "but it's looking likely he was an accomplice, yes."

"Which means I was what? Just an alibi?" Daisy asked.

"Perhaps," the detective mused, talking around the huge piece of jam, cream and scone, "tell me again what happened at the pub. If I recall correctly, your previous statements focused on what you saw just before, during and after the collision."

Daisy sighed, but took a sip of the cup of tea that had just appeared in front of her, gave Jacob a glare that she hoped warned the cat off jumping onto her lap, and began to rehash what she felt she had repeated many times, "I got to the pub at the arranged time..."

"Was Glendinning already there?" Cluero interrupted.

"Ah yes, he was at the table already, we ordered drinks…"

"What did he have? Was he on the heavy stuff?"

"Ah no, actually, he said he wasn't drinking because he was driving. So, I…"

"And yet he walked out and across the bridge. Didn't leave by car?" The detective sat up straighter, his weary eyes more alive than Daisy had hitherto seen them.

"Oh! Well, no," Daisy had that anxious feeling once again. The small niggle that she knew could build and explode so rapidly.

"Tell me, Daisy, and think carefully, did you see anyone leave as you arrived?"

"No, no, well except for Billy the pub's owner…" Daisy prayed for a revelation. Some memory that she had so far neglected, "but he did have an empty glass on the table next to him as if someone was not long departed. And I can tell you, Gemma is a stickler for clearing those tables…"

"So, just to confirm, it seems Glendinning had driven to the place with someone who was not there for you to meet, intending to walk home afterwards. Or, more accurately, to be in a certain place at a certain time with none other than the parish vicar as witness to his innocence," Cluero was already getting his phone out as he spoke, his scone long forgotten. An officer was dispatched to question the landlady at the Crow's Nest and the detective asked Daisy to repeat her statement more formally so that he could write it down.

"I guess I was played," Daisy said dolefully, after going through everything again, "and I think I can believe it of the man, but not of his mother. I've known Violet for a very long time, and I just don't think she would collude on murdering someone..."

Daisy explained about the treasure hunting then – only as far as it pertained to Jugger and Glendinning, she was very careful to leave Bunch and the tunnels out of it, "So I can see why Anthony might want the man out of the way, but what was in it for Violet? A new steam train for the town? Why would she have such a personal interest in that? Besides, she's never come across as violent – I mean, she wants me gone but she hasn't dispatched me back to our Maker herself!"

"Money maybe, fame and glory at the discovery of the treasure? Anyway, I shouldn't speculate," Cluero said, standing, "I'd better be off, need to bring her back in for questioning..."

Daisy showed the detective out with a heavy heart. It just didn't make sense. Not that she liked the haughty parishioner, but she couldn't bear the thought of Violet being unjustly accused. As Bunch had proven, a sense of justice ran deep with the vicar.

But with the almost indisputable evidence against her neighbour, and from her own son of all people, what could Daisy possibly do?

20. I THINK I'VE FOUND THE CULPRIT!

Tallie slept the rest of the day away, so grateful was she for a proper bed and a full stomach. When Joe arrived with the young woman's things later that evening, Daisy took it upon herself to shove the whole lot into the washing machine with the load that still sat in the basket. Not wanting to overstep any boundaries, Daisy didn't look through her guest's clothes, simply bundling them up and putting them all on to wash.

Sylvia had left the vicar to her privacy when the detective was there, and had become invested in a feature length Columbo movie, so Daisy knew she wouldn't see the housekeeper until it was time to heat up the shepherd's pie that they were having for tea.

Bunch's mention of Daisy's unrelenting search for justice for Gran, along with the reminder of her mum's death by a hit and run driver, had left the vicar with some unsettling questions. Since Sylvia had been her grandmother's best friend, Daisy wondered if she might have some answers and so waited impatiently for the TV show to finish.

"What's got you so antsy?" Sylvia asked when she eventually came through to the kitchen, followed by a trio of impatient pets who all sensed it was time for their evening meal.

"Actually, I was wanting to have a quick chat if that's okay?" Daisy said, putting the dish into the oven and sitting back down at the table.

"Aye lass, wanting to talk through the details of the murder with me, are you? Keen for an unbiased point of view?" Sylvia replied, unable to hide the gleeful anticipation in her voice.

"Ah no, not really, it's actually about Gran."

"Ah petal, I'm not sure there's anything left to talk about that night that we haven't gone over a million times…"

"No, not that night, I mean before then. I was

wondering if she ever confided in you?"

"Well we were best friends," the housekeeper hedged, not looking nearly as keen to chat now and glancing towards the oven as if for an excuse to leave the conversation.

"I know, so I'm guessing she told you things... things that she wouldn't share with a teenager."

"Probably, yes, but..."

"To be more specific," Daisy took a deep breath before continuing, "I was wondering if she'd told you who my father was? You must know it was what she and I had been arguing about around the time of her death. That I wanted the information and she wouldn't share it."

"Your father? Where has this come from, Daisy? You never had a father."

"Well, yes, obviously I know that, but there must've been a man in the picture originally. Do you remember my mum being in a relationship?"

"She was so young and it was so long ago... the broccoli needs chopping."

"Leave the veg," Daisy heard her own raised voice and

struggled to keep her emotions in check, "please Sylvia, I know there's no father's name on my birth certificate, but did Gran tell you who it was? Was there gossip in the town? How long was he with my mum? Did he come to her funeral after the hit and run?"

"Daisy, lass, please," Sylvia put her hand over the vicar's where it rested on top of the table, "there's no good can come from revisiting the past, believe me."

Daisy looked into the older woman's face then, really looked, and was shocked by what she saw. Even under the make-up, Sylvia's face was white and clammy, her hand too felt sweaty and it made the vicar wonder what the woman was hiding... and why. She seemed... well, scared, if Daisy wasn't mistaken.

"I hope I'm not interrupting..." Tallie hovered in the doorway, looking only slightly less fragile after her long nap.

"Not at all," Sylvia practically jumped from her chair, rushing into the boot room to put distance between herself and Daisy, clearly grateful for the excuse to end the conversation.

We'll definitely be revisiting that soon, the vicar thought to herself as a shriek came from the adjoining room.

"I just don't understand why you would put coloureds in with whites," Sylvia was lamenting, as she held up the pile of blouses and undies which were now dyed pink, "Aha! I think I've found the culprit!" The housekeeper had been sifting through the basket of wet clothes which sat on the kitchen table – to the apparent horror of their guest who was backed up against the kitchen door, wide-eyed and open-mouthed. Indeed, the young woman gasped as Sylvia produced a small, red item with a flourish. It seemed to have shrunk in the wash, but without doubt Daisy recognised it as the hat Violet had been wearing to Sunday service before something fitting that description had been seen on Jugger's killer in the woman's own car.

Tallie turned to flee with a sob, only to be met in the hallway by Cluero, who had let himself in.

"We really need to start locking that door," Daisy exclaimed, though only to divert her mind from the horrible realisation that they had inadvertently found the driver of the car that had mowed down Jugger.

"A few words, if you don't mind," the Welshman held Tallie gently by the elbow and escorted her back into the kitchen, "I hear from the landlady that you had a drink with your boyfriend at the pub the other day…"

"So, that wrong'un Anthony used the spare key to his mother's car, drove to the pub, met that poor lass and persuaded her to mow down that awful man wearing his mother's hat that still sat on the dashboard after church. And then had the gall to blame his own mother!" Sylvia shook her head as if in disbelief.

"It would seem so, yes," Daisy sighed into her cup of chamomile tea and wished she could just go to bed. This had been an interminably long day, topped off by the shock of seeing Tallie led away in handcuffs, and the vicar couldn't even think straight any longer.

"But why would she do that? She had her whole life ahead of her."

Daisy thought of Tallie's abuse at Jugger's hands, of his baby that the young woman reluctantly carried and her desire to escape his clutches, but said none of it, replying simply, "She was desperate."

"I'm guessing he told her when to set off from his parents' house after he left you in the pub and spotted the victim ambling along," Sylvia was back in investigative mode and Daisy was too tired to do anything but nod, "Goodness me, what an outcome. That poor girl."

"Indeed," the legs of Daisy's chair screeched against

the hard floor as she stood as briskly as she could manage, "such a sad situation."

The housekeeper nodded as Daisy left the room, whilst the vicar herself wondered – not for the first time – why an all-loving God would allow such bad things to happen to innocent people.

Free will, she told herself, but again not for the first time the explanation rang hollow in her own ears.

21. A FORCE TO BE RECKONED WITH

It was a vicar heavy in body and spirit who chose to hide away in her tiny church office the next morning. She had been plagued with nightmares all night long – of her own mother's fatal accident, but showing Tallie at the wheel of the car – past and present intertwining as they so often did in her head, and Daisy felt nauseous from it all. Therefore when a soft knock came on the door, Daisy hunched down in her chair and pretended not to be there.

"Daisy, love, Sylvia said you were in here," the familiar face of Gerald Bunch peered around the door, opening it a crack, giving the vicar no choice but to invite him in.

The room was cramped as it was, being a converted cupboard, and housing simply a desk, one chair and a filing cabinet, so there was nowhere for the tall, lanky man to perch. Instead he towered over Daisy for a second, until even he must have felt the situation uncomfortable and so dropped to one knee in front of her, bringing his eyes level with the vicar's.

The scene was now all-too reminiscent of a proposal and Daisy felt her stomach begin to churn as she watched a single bead of sweat trail down the man's forehead. Bunch too, must've realised the symbolism of his stance and so changed to be balancing on his haunches – decidedly more wobbly, but much more acceptable, Daisy thought to herself.

Clearly the position was slightly uncomfortable for him, as Bunch launched quickly into what sounded like a previously prepared and well-rehearsed speech, "Daisy Bloom, I think you must know that my feelings for you go beyond friendship. What started as a ruse to add another layer to my disguise has turned into true and deep feelings. I can't tell you how sorry I am about the other day, it has given me much to think on and I can say with genuine sincerity that if you ask it of me I will set aside my obsession with the tunnels and treasures of Lillymouth and focus on floristry. After all, I have found that I have a natural talent at the profession that was meant to be merely a front for…"

"Gerald," Daisy interrupted him there. The poor man was awash with sweat and about to tip over sideways. At the beginning of his declaration, Bunch had taken both of Daisy's hands in his, and she used these now to encourage the man to stand up again, joining him on her feet and moving to the side to put some distance between them.

"Gerald," she repeated, taking the moment to gather her thoughts, "you asked me the other evening if I could give up my search for Gran's killer. Like you, I have thought on this and the honest answer is no, I can't stop seeking justice until the murderer is found and behind bars. I'm sorry, I…"

"Please don't apologise, love, I wasn't going to ask that of you. We can investigate together, I can protect you from Briggs. He's been far too quiet recently, making me think he's plotting his revenge in the background. Your safety is my primary…"

Daisy sighed and squeezed the man's hands which seemed to have found their way into hers again. Looking into his eyes she saw nothing but earnest admiration there and it made what the vicar was about to say all the harder.

"Gerald, ah Marcus, I feel I should use your real name now as we are stripping back the formalities and untruths and being totally honest with each other. Marcus, I have spent my whole adult life thinking I would remain single till the end of my days. Having witnessed some of the worst of humanity over the years, I never had cause to question this decision. Nor was I presented with any temptation to do so. That being said, there is no switch inside me which I flicked to feel that way, and therefore no way to turn off…"

"Sorry to interrupt you, but you've just mentioned temptation, and perhaps the switch has been changed by itself… I mean, in the course of our getting to know each other?" The desperation in his voice was clear now and Daisy felt like a horrible person for squashing his hope.

"Marcus, you're right, perhaps I have some feelings for you that go beyond friendship, I can't deny that. However, the real question is whether, at this time, I want to explore them and I'm afraid the answer to that is no. I'm on a path that is mine alone to walk and I fear it's going to get much worse before it gets better. I won't ask anyone to join me on that."

"But you wouldn't be asking, I would be offering…"

"Marcus, you are my best friend in this town, please

can we keep it that way? Does there need to be awkwardness between us?"

The man sighed heavily and leaned forward to peck Daisy on the forehead, "No, no there doesn't. Friends it is then."

Daisy was still ruminating on the exchange with Bunch, wondering why her head felt clearer yet her heart even heavier after their conversation, when there came another knock on the office door. This one decidedly more aggressive.

"Come in," Daisy had given up on having any private time that morning, apparently her housekeeper was sending the whole village across here. The vicar knew that thought was unfair, but her mood was fragile and her temper even more so, and it was this which caused her to groan out loud when it was Violet Glendinning who stalked into the room.

"If you've come to thank me for proving your innocence, there's no need," Daisy decided a pre-emptive strike was in order, "it was purely accidental, nothing deliberate on my part."

"Thank you?" The woman's voice was so high it

bordered on hysterical, "Thank you? My goodness what a strange view of the world you have, Daisy Bloom. Why would I thank you for getting my son locked up when it was that little trollop who was to blame..."

"Excuse me?" Daisy stood quickly using the desk for support, the full force of her indignation filling those two words, "How dare you! That young woman that you so rudely refer to is a vulnerable victim of abuse and manipulation who your son saw fit to use in his quest to get rid of a rival. I doubt she even knew what she was doing after your son plied her with alcohol and promises, shoved your car keys into her hand and sent her to do his dirty work. I imagine life has given her few options and your precious son stole even more of them from her. Don't come to me with your accusations and self-righteousness, Violet, it stinks more than that waiting room that Tallie was forced to live in."

"Well, I... I mean..."

"Yes, I know exactly what you meant. Now, if that is all?"

Daisy felt her legs shaking as the door slammed and she sank back into her chair. Perhaps the esteemed Mrs. Glendinning would think twice before confronting her again – or at least that was what Daisy hoped, now that she had proved that the Daisy Bloom who had come back to Lillymouth was no shrinking violet. Gone was the scared girl who had fled under a black cloud. Gone was the woman who returned to the town seeking to fit in and keep her head down. This was the real Daisy, and she was a force to be reckoned with.

22. A PERFECT DAY

It was a beautiful summer's day on the North
Yorkshire coast. The kind of weather that brought out
the best in the small town of Lillymouth and its
inhabitants. In the past months the old train station
had been brought back to life, the waiting room and
platforms returned to their former glory, and a vintage
steam engine and carriage brought onto the track. The
sun glinted off the metalwork, the children squealed as
the driver hooted the horn signalling it was time for
boarding, and the bunting swayed gently in the small
breeze that came from the North Sea.

Reverend Daisy Bloom watched happily as families
climbed aboard for the inaugural trip a mile down the
track and back, accepting the hot tea in a cardboard

cup which her best friend, Gerald Bunch, offered her. Bought from the refreshment kiosk run by Bea and Andrew, which served drinks and snacks and sold books and postcards, just as the vicar had suggested all those months ago.

It was a perfect day. The last one in Daisy's memory in fact, before the most tumultuous and testing time of her life began. Oh, how Daisy wished she could return to that day. The day before it all started. The day before she was accused of murder...

The shocking finale of the Lillymouth Mysteries trilogy will be published in October 2023, and Reverend Daisy will need all the support she can get if she is to escape unscathed.

"Chin Up Buttercup" Lillymouth Mysteries Book 3

Have you visited Flora Miller, her feisty feathered friend and the residents of Baker's Rise yet? If not, read on for an excerpt from the first book in the series, "Here Today, Scone Tomorrow."

R. A. Hutchins

23. EXCERPT FROM "HERE TODAY, SCONE TOMORROW – BAKER'S RISE MYSTERIES BOOK ONE"

Stan Houghton stormed out of the front door of the manor house known as 'The Rise' and strode off down the gravel driveway. His face, a molten red from his latest showdown with the 'lord of the manor' Harold Baker, contorted into a furious visage which matched his balled fists and heavy breathing. Surprised to see a familiar figure, dressed to the nines, approaching from the other direction, Stan tried to rein in his temper whilst making pleasantries.

"Good morning, Mrs. Edwards, fine day," he did not pause even for a second as they passed each other, nor did Stan listen for a reply as he hurried off back to the farm.

"If that's you again Houghton, you can get lost!" the shouted warning from indoors could be heard behind the flaking wooden main door of the manor, as its next visitor waited patiently on the doorstep.

"Oh, hello," his greeting was hardly welcoming even when Harold did pull the door open, "you'd better come in then!" He stalked into the main drawing room, eyeing his pet parrot suspiciously as if an outburst might ensue, and muttering, "not a word," as Harold waggled his finger in the direction of his feathered friend's perch.

The parrot, taking only one fleeting look at the outstretched finger, and choosing to also ignore the hastily given warning completely, screeched, "Old trout! Old trout!" and rose from his perch, flapping his wings viciously around the head of the woman who had just entered the room.

"Enough!" Harold said sternly, and the parrot finally decided to cease his assault.

"I gather this isn't a great time? I suppose Farmer Houghton was commenting on your latest rent increases for the village?" The woman tried surreptitiously to restore the elaborate up-do which the stupid parrot had managed to make look like a bird's nest. Giving up, she continued, "With the number of fields he has, I'd wager he's sorely affected." She stated it as a matter of fact, apparently unmoved by either the rent situation or the plight of a neighbour.

"Aye, well, he's always here threatening when the prices go up, but he pays it in the end. Just like they all do, if they want to keep living in Baker's Rise."

"Quite so. Anyhow, I've been baking and thought you might like a scone or two?"

Harold tried to hide his surprise. It was not a common occurrence for villagers to make their way up the hill for anything other than to air their gripes, let alone such a comely example of womanhood. For a moment, Harold was lost in sweet reminiscence of his many dalliances in years gone by. He was old now, stout in the waist and grizzly of feature, so he very much doubted that was what was on offer here. Nevertheless, he was intrigued as to what exactly would warrant such a special visit.

"Thank you kindly, dear lady, please take a seat and I will prepare a pot of tea," Harold licked his lips as he took in the sight of her, her face all made up to show her features at their best, her body encased in a tight tweed suit. When the lady didn't immediately sit, he was confused for a moment, until he realised that she would need to perch on top of one of the many mounds of paperwork, old magazines and newspapers which littered every available surface. Quickly, Harold swept a pile of brochures from the end of a settee and rushed off to the kitchen.

When he returned, the scones were arranged on one of the fine china plates, inherited from his mother, and which were stored in glass-fronted cabinets all around the room. Jam and butter – which she must have brought with her – sat in two dainty dishes complete with a miniature silver spoon and knife. Aye, she's after something, Harold thought to himself, his mind whirring with what he might get in return, as he set the tray on the small walnut coffee table between them, also cleared of its mound of papers hastily, and took his usual seat on a sagging Chesterfield.

"Shall I be mother?" she said coyly, fluttering her eyelashes at him.

Harold almost blushed like a schoolboy, "Indeed, madam, thank you kindly."

As she poured the tea and added the five sugar cubes which he requested, Harold thought he detected a small tremor in the lady's hands. Assuming it was a nervous anticipation for what was surely about to pass between them, Harold bestowed upon her his most gracious smile, which some rather ungrateful females had in the past told him more resembled a leer. Accepting the cup and saucer gratefully, and the proffered scone, Harold settled back into his chair.

"So, my dear, what brings you up here?"

Instead of answering, the woman simply looked on as Harold's hand reached to his mouth and he took a huge bite of the baked treat.

"You do," she whispered, as Harold felt his breath begin to shorten, his chest to tighten, his tongue to swell and his throat to close.

The dropped plate smashed on the parquet floor, as Harold grasped his throat and managed to gargle, "What the..?" He staggered towards his guest, who simply moved out of his range.

"Peanut," she spoke clearly and with a sadistic smile, as Harold noticed for the first time the smudge of bright red lipstick on the woman's teeth, as if it had been applied by someone unused to doing so. It made her look like one of those clowns in a horror film. Why he would notice that, of all things now, Harold wondered as he collapsed to the floor, his body convulsing.

The last things he saw were her stilettoed feet stepping over him as the woman went to retrieve the rest of the scones, and the china cups and saucers for washing. She reached down to check Harold's pulse, giving a nod of approval as she found none, before quickly collecting up the fallen remnants along with the broken pieces of crockery, and leaving the room silently.

Nought could be heard but the ticking of the antique Grandfather clock in the corner and the squawk of the parrot, shouting "Peanut" on repeat.

Ten Months Later

Flora looked around her at the six small tables, all set out with fine china cups and saucers in co-ordinating colours, lace doilies, floral tablecloths and silver cutlery. She smiled to herself, content in all she had achieved since coming to Baker's Rise a few months ago. The tearoom in the old stables, closed up for several years, had been given a new lease of life with a fresh lick of paint and bunting hung around the rough walls. A new sign had been hung outside the door, advertising the 'Tearoom on The Rise' – Flora liked to keep things simple and elegant. She ran her hands down her smart apron and patted her hair to ensure she was as smart as possible, before checking her watch for the fifth time in as many minutes. Still half an hour remained till opening time. The local baker, George Jones, had dropped off the day's delicacies an hour ago, and Flora had already arranged them in the display cabinet and fridge. Scones with clotted cream from the local farm and jam from the farm shop, teacakes, iced buns, custard tarts… a whole list of tempting treats for what Flora hoped would be her many customers, keen to try out the new tearoom on opening day. Flora wished to be baking some of the goods herself before too long, once she'd found someone in the village to teach her. She would start out as easily as possible, she had decided, and try to perfect the traditional English scone.

Flora had advertised the tearoom's opening in the local parish newsletter, the aptly titled, "What's on the Rise in Baker's Rise," as well as on the church notice board. She had tried to spread the news by word of mouth too, though this was more difficult as Flora was new to the village. She had quickly realised that folk here were not too keen on newcomers. Trust had to be earned, and civility only turned to friendship when you had embedded yourself suitably in village life. Flora hoped desperately that this would be a quicker process for her than for most, since she wished the tearoom to become a hub of village life. Mindful that any customers would have to travel halfway up the small hill, The Rise, to reach her, she had already thought about special offers and loyalty schemes to tempt people her way. Probably getting ahead of herself, Flora knew, but after coming from a fast-paced and highly structured job in the city, she was already struggling to fill her days and occupy her quick mind.

The bell on the door chimed and Flora was shocked from her musings. It was still too early for customers.

"Flora? Are you here?" The polished tone of the local solicitor, Harry Bentley, put Flora at her ease as she rushed from behind the counter to greet him. His grey hair popped around the door which he had only opened a fraction, followed by his wide-rimmed spectacles and his red, bulbous nose.

"Harry! What a lovely surprise!" the elderly gent, who should have been long since retired by now but still took an interest in the affairs of the village residents, had been Flora's sole friend and confidant since she'd arrived. It was he who had originally contacted her about the estate, he who had advised she should keep her true identity a secret until she had been accepted by the villagers. Harry had arranged the refurbishment of the coach house for Flora per her instructions from London, and had suggested the tearoom as a viable business opportunity. He had met her when she arrived and had visited her several times since, always with a friendly smile and a word of advice.

"Just thought I'd come to wish you luck on your first day, dear! Well, doesn't it look splendid! Very pretty indeed."

"Oh thank you, Harry, it wouldn't be anything without your recommendations and advice. Thank you for suggesting the farm shop, by the way, the jam and honey is delicious!"

"Not at all, my dear, now where are we with all the paperwork up at the big house?"

"Well, as you know there is mounds of it, I have only been able to shift the tip of the iceberg really. I know, it's my own fault. Being an actuary for so many years, I can't throw a single sheet of paper away without first reading what's on it! It makes the process slow and laborious, but I'm not in a hurry. The whole place is becoming dilapidated anyway. As you know, I've used the funds I could get my hands on to do up the coach house and this stable block. I'll have to wait to receive my divorce settlement before I can begin anything else. Hopefully, the villagers will have accepted me by then and it won't need to be so cloak and dagger," she gave a rueful smile and offered Harry a coffee from the new machine, which Flora had only just begun to learn how to use.

Eyeing the large silver monstrosity with distrust, Harry opted for a cup of tea, and sat down at the table nearest the counter.

"Aye, you've accomplished a lot in a few months, slow and steady wins the race especially in a place like Baker's Rise!"

"Indeed," Flora joined him at the table, a pot of tea for two and two toasted teacakes set in front of them. They chatted happily, until Flora looked at her watch and realised she should have changed the small sign on the door to 'open' some fifteen minutes ago. Not that she need worry, it was hardly as if she had a queue of customers waiting outside.

"I'll go and leave you to it. Remember to phone me if you need anything. On my home phone, mind, I still haven't worked out this mobile thing that my nephew gave me."

"Thank you, Harry," Flora busied herself clearing the table as she heard Harry's old BMW driving away on the gravel driveway. She took a deep breath, closed her eyes, and prayed that luck would be on her side and bring her some customers on her first day.

Chin Up Buttercup

The Lillymouth Mysteries Book Three

Coming October 6th 2023

The shocking finale of the Lillymouth Mysteries trilogy is here, and Reverend Daisy will need all the support she can get if she is to escape unscathed.

A late night arrival leads a reluctant Daisy to the crime scene of another murder. Unfortunately for the vicar, she recognises the body as a longtime foe and kneeling beside the deceased is definitely the last place she should be found.

Quickly realising she has been set up, Daisy must uncover the identity of her backstabbing adversary before it's too late. Has she been altogether too trusting of those around her? Has she underestimated her haters in the parish? Or is the answer to another secret about to be revealed?

Not knowing who to trust, Daisy shuns all help, deciding to go it alone this time. Will this prove to be a costly mistake or a wise choice? Only time will tell.

And the clock is ticking.

R. A. Hutchins

ABOUT THE AUTHOR

Rachel Hutchins lives in northeast England with her husband, three children and their dog Boudicca. She loves writing both mysteries and romances, and enjoys reading these genres too. Her favourite place is walking along the local coastline, with a coffee and some cake!

You can connect with Rachel and sign up to her quarterly **newsletter** via her website at: www.authorrachelhutchins.com

Alternatively, she has social media pages on:

Facebook: www.facebook.com/rahutchinsauthor

Instagram: www.instagram.com/ra_hutchins_author

R. A. Hutchins

OTHER MYSTERY BOOKS BY R. A. HUTCHINS

Here Today, Scone Tomorrow

Baker's Rise Mysteries Book One

When the self-titled Lord of the Manor, Harold Baker, meets an untimely end, the residents of Baker's Rise believe that he has simply died from choking. It is fair to say that they are certainly not sad to see him go!

Former city dweller Flora Miller, new to the quaint English village and in charge of the recently restored Tearoom on the Rise, is the unlucky recipient of the late man's parrot. Her new feathered companion has no filter and a vibrant personality that cannot be ignored! Witness to Harold's murder, the bird won't let the matter lie, and it's not long before Flora becomes suspicious.

A quest to bake the perfect scone is put on hold whilst Flora helps the charming Detective Bramble to investigate Harold's death. She has set her hopes on writing the next bestseller, not on becoming an amateur sleuth, but life sometimes has surprises in store!

Will they find the killer before they strike again, and can Flora find the acceptance and friendship she seeks amongst her new neighbours?

Packed with twists and turns, colourful characters and a sprinkle of romance, this is the first book in the series of Baker's Rise Mysteries. It will certainly leave you hungry for more!

(Includes a traditional scone recipe!)

There are currently nine books available in this series.

ROMANCES BY THIS AUTHOR

The Angel and the Wolf

What do a beautiful recluse, a well-trained husky, and a middle-aged biker have in common?
Find out in this poignant story of love and hope!

When Isaac meets the Angel and her Wolf, he's unsure whether he's in Hell or Heaven.
Worse still, he can't remember taking that final step.
They say that calm follows the storm, but will that be the case for Isaac?

Fate has led him to her door,
Will she have the courage to let him in?

To Catch A Feather
Found in Fife Book One

When tragedy strikes an already vulnerable Kate Winters, she retreats into herself, broken and beaten. Existing rather than living, she makes a journey North to try to find herself, or maybe just looking for some sort of closure.

Cameron McAllister has known his own share of grief and love lost. His son, Josh, is now his only priority. In his forties and running a small coffee shop in a tiny Scottish fishing village, Cal knows he is unlikely to find love again.

When the two meet and sparks fly, can they overcome their past losses and move on towards a shared future, or are the memories which haunt them still too real?

These books, as well as others by Rachel, can be found on Amazon worldwide in e-book and paperback formats, as well as free to read on Kindle Unlimited.

Printed in Great Britain
by Amazon

46353587R00116